The Heart
of Una Sackville

Mrs. George de Horne Vaizey

Chapter One.

May 13th, 1895.

Lena Streatham gave me this diary. I can't think what possessed her, for she has been simply hateful to me sometimes this last term. Perhaps it was remorse, because it's awfully handsome, with just the sort of back I like—soft Russia leather, with my initials in the corner, and a clasp with a dear little key, so that you can leave it about without other people seeing what is inside. I always intended to keep a diary when I left school and things began to happen, and I suppose I must have said so some day; I generally do blurt out what is in my mind, and Lena heard and remembered. She's not a bad girl, except for her temper, but I've noticed the hasty o nes are generally the most generous. There are hundreds and hundreds of leaves in it, and I expect it will be years before it's finished. I'm not going to write things every day—that's silly! I'll just keep it for times when I want to talk, and Lorna is not near to confide in. It's quite exciting to think all that will be written in these empty pages! What fun it would be if I could read them now and see what is going to happen! About half way through I shall be engaged, and in the last page of all I'll scribble a few words in my wedding-dress before I go on to church, for that will be the end of Una Sackville, and there will be nothing more to write after that. It's very nice to be married, of course, but stodgy—there's no more excitement.

There has been plenty of excitement to-day, at any rate. I always thought it would be lovely when the time came for leaving school, and having nothing to do but enjoy oneself, but I've cried simply bucketfuls, and my head aches like fury. All the girls were so fearfully nice. I'd no idea they liked me so much. Irene May began crying at breakfast-time, and one or another of them has been at it the whole day long. Maddie made me walk with her in the crocodile, and said, "Croyez bien, ma chérie, que votre Maddie ne vous oubliera jamais." It's all very well, but she's been a perfect pig to me many times over about the irregular verbs! She gave me her

1

photograph in a gilt frame—not half bad; you would think she was quite nice-looking.

The kiddies joined together and gave me a purse—awfully decent of the poor little souls—and I've got simply dozens of books and ornaments and little picture things for my room. We had cake for tea, but half the girls wouldn't touch it. Florence said it was sickening to gorge when your heart was breaking. She is going to ask her mother to let her leave next term, for she says she simply cannot stand our bedroom after I'm gone. She and Lorna don't get on a bit, and I was always having to keep the peace. I promised faithfully I would write sheets upon sheets to them every single week, because my leaving at half term makes it harder for them than if they were going home too.

"We shall be so flat and dull without you, Circle!" Myra said. She calls me "Circle" because I'm fat—not awfully, you know, but just a little bit, and she's so thin herself. "I think I'll turn over a new leaf and go in for work. I don't seem to have any heart for getting into scrapes by myself!"

"Well, we *have* kept them going, haven't we!" I said. "Do you remember," and then we talked over the hairbreadth escapes we had had, and groaned to think that the good times were passed.

"I will say this for Una," said Florence, "however stupid she may be at lessons, I never met a girl who was cleverer at scenting a joke!"

When Florence says a thing, she *means* it, so it was an awful compliment, and I was just trying to look humble when Mary came in to say Miss Martin wanted me in the drawing-room. I did feel bad, because I knew it would be our last real talk, and she looked simply sweet in her new blue dress and her Sunday afternoon expression. She can look as fierce as anything and snap your head off if you vex her, but she's a darling all the same, and I adore her. She's been perfectly sweet to me these three years, and we have had lovely talks sometimes—serious talks, I mean—when I was going to be confirmed, and when father was ill, and when I've been homesick.

She's so good, but not a bit goody, and she makes you long to be good too. She's just the right person to have a girls' school, for she understands how girls feel, and that it isn't natural for them to be solemn, unless of course they are prigs, and they don't count.

I sat down beside her and we talked for an hour. I wish I could remember all the things she said, and put them down here to be my rules for life, but it's so difficult to remember.

She said my gaiety and lightness of heart had been a great help to them all, and like sunshine in the school. Of course, it had led me into scrapes at times, but they had been innocent and kindly, and so she had not been hard upon me. But now I was grown up and going out into the battle of life, and everything was different.

"You know, dear, the gifts which God gives us are our equipments for that fight, and I feel sure your bright, happy disposition has been given to you to help you in some special needs of life."

I didn't quite like her saying that! It made me feel creepy, as if horrid things were going to happen, and I should need my spirit to help me through. I want to be happy and have a good time. I never can understand how people can bear troubles, and illnesses, and being poor, and all those awful things. I should die at once if they happened to me.

She went on to say that I must make up my mind from the first not to live for myself; that it was often a very trying time when a girl first left school and found little or nothing to occupy her energies at home, but that there were so many sad and lonely people in the world that no one need ever feel any lack of a purpose in life, and she advised me not to look at charity from a general standpoint, but to narrow it down till it came within my own grasp.

"Don't think vaguely of the poor all over the world; think of one person at your own gate, and brighten that life. I once heard a very good man say that the only way he could reconcile himself to the seeming injustice between the lots of the poor and the rich was by believing that each of the latter was deputed by God to look after his poorer brother, and was *responsible* for his welfare. Find someone whom you can take to your heart as your poor sister in God's great family, and help her in every way you can. It will keep you from growing selfish and worldly. In your parents' position you will, of course, go a great deal into society and be admired and made much of, as a bright, pretty girl. It is only natural that you should enjoy the experience, but don't let it turn your head. Try to keep your frank, unaffected manners, and be honest in words and actions. Be especially careful not to be led away by greed of power and admiration. It is the best thing that can happen to any woman to win the love of a good, true man, but it is cruel to wreck his happiness to gratify a foolish vanity. I hope that none of my girls may be so forgetful of all that is true and womanly."

She looked awfully solemn. I wonder if she flirted when she was young, and he was furious and went away and left her! We always wondered why she didn't marry. There's a photograph of a man on her writing-table, and Florence said she is sure that was him, for he is in such a lovely frame, and she puts the best flowers beside him like a shrine.

Florence is awfully clever at making up tales. She used to tell us them in bed, (like that creature with the name in the *Arabian Nights*). We used to say:

"Now then, Florence, go on—tell us Fraulein's love-story!" and she would clear her throat, and cough, and say—"It was a glorious summer afternoon in the little village of Eisenach, and the sunshine peering down through the leaves turned to gold the tresses of young Elsa Behrend as she sat knitting under the trees."

It was just like a book, and so true too, for Fraulein is always knitting! The Romance de Mademoiselle was awfully exciting. There was a duel in it, and one man was killed and the other had to run away, so she got neither of them, and it was that that soured her temper.

I really must go to bed—Lorna keeps calling and calling—and Florence is crying still—I can hear her sniffing beneath the clothes. We shall be perfect wrecks in the morning, and mother won't like it if I go home a fright. Heigho! the very last night in this dear old room! I hate the last of anything—even nasty things—and except when we've quarrelled we've had jolly times. It's awful to think I shall never be a school-girl any more! I don't believe I shall sleep a wink all night. I feel wretched.

PS—Fancy calling me pretty! I'm so pleased. I shall look nicer still in my new home clothes.

Chapter Two.

Bed-time; my own room. May 14th.

It is different from school! My room is simply sweet, all newly done up as a surprise for me on my return. White paint and blue walls, and little bookcases in the corners, and comfy chairs and cushions, and a writing-table, and such lovely artistic curtains—dragons making faces at fleur-de-lys on a dull blue background. I'm awfully well off, and they are all so good to me, I ought to be the happiest girl in the world, but I feel sort of achey and strange, and a little bit lonely, though I wouldn't say so for the world. I miss the girls.

It was awful this morning—positively awful. I should think there was a flood after I left—all the girls howled so, and I was sticking my head out of the carriage window all the journey to get my face cool before I arrived. Father met me at the station, and we spanked up together in the dog-cart. That was scrumptious. I do love rushing through the air behind a horse like Firefly, and father is such an old love, and always understands how you feel. He is very quiet and shy, and when anyone else is there he hardly speaks a word, but we chatter like anything when we are together. I have a kind of idea that he likes me best, though Spencer and Vere are the show members of the family. Spencer is the heir, and is almost always away because he is a soldier, and Vere is away a lot too, because she hates the country, and likes visiting about and having a good time. She's awfully pretty, but—No! I won't say it. I hereby solemnly vow and declare that I shall never say nasty things of anyone in this book, only, of course, if they do nasty things, I shall have to tell, or it won't be true. She isn't much with father, anyway, and he likes to be made a fuss of, because he's so quiet himself. Isn't it funny how people are like that! You'd think they'd like you to be prim and quiet too, but they don't a bit, and the more you plague them the better they're pleased.

"Back again, my girl, are you? A finished young lady, eh?" said father, flicking his whip.

"Very glad of it, I can tell you. I'm getting old, and need someone to look after me a bit." He looked me up and down, with a sort of anxious look, as if he wanted to see if I were changed. "We had good times together when you were a youngster and used to trot round with me every morning to see the dogs and the horses, but I suppose you won't care for that sort of thing now. It will be all dresses and running about from one excitement to another. You won't care for tramping about in thick boots with the old father!"

I laughed, and pinched him in his arm. "Don't fish! You know very well I'll like it better than anything else. Of course, I shall like pretty dresses too, and as much fun as I can get, but I don't think I shall ever grow up properly, father—enough to walk instead of run, and smile sweetly instead of shrieking with laughter as we do at school. It will be a delightful way of letting off steam to go off with you for some long country rambles, and have some of our nice old talks."

He turned and stared at me quite hard, and for a long time. He has such a lot of wrinkles round his eyes, and they look so tired. I never noticed it before. He looked sort of sad, and as if he wanted something. I wonder if he has been lonely while I was away. Poor old dad! I'll be a perfect angel to him. I'll never neglect him for my own amusement like Resolution number one! Sentence can't be finished.

"How old are you, child?" father said at last, turning away with a sigh and flicking Firefly gently with the whip, and I sat up straight and said proudly—

"Nearly nineteen. I begged to stay on another half year, you know, because of the exam, but I failed again in that hateful arithmetic: I'm a perfect dunce over figures, father; I hope you don't mind. I can sing very well; my voice was better than any of the other girls, and that will give you more pleasure than if I could do all the sums in the world. They tried to teach me algebra, too. Such a joke; I once got an equation right. The teacher nearly had a fit. It was the most awful fluke."

"I don't seem to care much about your arithmetical prowess," father said, smiling. "I shall not ask you to help me with my accounts, but it will be a pleasure to hear you sing, especially if you will indulge me with a ballad now and then which I can really enjoy. You are older than I thought; but keep as young as you can, child. I don't want to lose my little playfellow yet awhile. I've missed her very badly these last years."

I liked to hear that. It was sad for him, of course, but I simply love people to love me and feel bad when I'm gone. I was far and away the most popular girl at school, but it wasn't all chance as they seemed to think. I'm sure I worked hard enough for the position. If a girl didn't like me I was so fearfully nice to her that she was simply forced to come round. I said something like that to Lorna once, and she was quite shocked, and called it self-seeking and greed for admiration, and all sorts of horrid names. I don't see it at all; I call it a most amiable weakness. It makes you pleasant and kind even if you feel horrid, and that must be nice. I felt all bubbling over with good resolutions when father said that, and begged him to let me be not only his playmate but his helper also, and to tell me at once what I could do.

He smiled again in that sad sort of way grown-up people have, which seems to say that they know such a lot more than you, and are sorry for your ignorance.

"Nothing definite, darling," he said; "an infinite variety of things indefinite! Love me, and remember me sometimes among the new distractions—that's about the best you can do;" and I laughed, and pinched him again.

"You silly old dear! As if I could ever forget!" and just at that moment we drove up to the porch.

If it had been another girl's mother, she would have been waiting at the door to receive me. I've been home with friends, so I know; but my mother is different. I don't think I should like it if she did come! It doesn't fit into my idea of her, some way. Mother is like a queen—

everyone waits upon her, and goes up to her presence like a throne-room. I peeped into the mirror in the hall as I passed, and tucked back some ends of hair, and straightened my tie, and then the door opened, and there she stood—the darling!—holding out her arms to welcome me, with her eyes all soft and tender, as they used to be when she came to say "good night." Mother is not demonstrative as a rule, so you simply love it when she is. She looks quite young, and she was the beauty of the county when she was a girl, and I never did see in all my life anybody so immaculately perfect in appearance! Her dresses fit as if she had been melted into them; her skirts stand out, and go crinkling in and out into folds just exactly like the fashion-plates; her hair looks as if it had been done a minute before—I don't believe she would have a single loose end if she were out in a tornado. It's the same, morning, noon and night; if she were wrecked on a desert island she would be a vision of elegance. It's the way she was born. I can't think how I came to be her daughter, and I know I'm a trial to her with my untidiness.

We hugged each other, and she put her hands on each side of my face, and we kissed and kissed again. She is taller than I am, and very dark, with beautiful aquiline features, and deep brown eyes. She is very slight—I'm sure my waist is about twice as big—and her hands look so pretty with the flashing rings. I'm awfully proud of my mother!

"My darling girl! How rejoiced I am to have you back. Sit down here and let me see you. How well you look, dear—not any thinner yet, I see! It will be delightful to have you at home for good, for Vere is away so much that I have felt quite bereft. Sit up, darling—don't stoop! It will be so interesting to have another girl to bring out! There are plenty of young people about here now, so you need not be dull, and I hope we shall be great companions. You were a sad little hoyden in the old days, but now that you have passed eighteen you will be glad to settle down, won't you, dear, and behave like the woman you are. Have you no little brooch, darling, to keep that collar straight at the neck? It is all adrift, and looks so untidy. Those little things are of such importance. I had such a charming letter from Miss Martin, full of nice speeches about you. She says you sing so sweetly. You must have some good lessons, for nothing is more taking than a young voice properly trained, and I hope you have no foolish nervousness about singing in public. You must get over it, if you have, for I rely on you to help me when we have visitors."

"I want to help you, mother. I will truly try," I said wistfully. I don't know why exactly, but I felt depressed all of a sudden. I wanted her to be so pleased at my return that she didn't notice anything but just me, and it hurt to be called to order so soon. I looked across the room, and caught a glimpse of our two figures reflected in a glass— such a big, fair, tousled creature as I looked beside her, and my heart went down lower then ever. I shall disappoint her, I know I shall! She expects me to be an elegant, accomplished young lady like Vere, and I feel a hoyden still, and not a bit a grown-up woman; besides, father said I was to keep young. How am I to please them both, and have time left over to remember Miss Martin's lessons? It strikes me, Una Sackville, you have got your work cut out.

Mother brought me up to see my room. She has looked after it all herself, and taken no end of trouble making the shades. It looked sweet in the sunshine, and I shall love sitting in the little round window writing my adventures in this book; but now that it's dark I miss the girls: I wonder what Lorna and Florence are doing now? Talking of me, I expect, and crying into their pillows. It seems years since we parted, and already I feel such miles apart. It seems almost impossible to believe that last night I was eating thick bread-and-butter for supper and lying down in the middle bed in the bare old dormitory. Now already I feel quite grown up and responsible. Oh, if I live to be a hundred years old, I shall never, never be at school again! I've been so happy. I wonder, I wonder shall I ever be as happy again?

Chapter Three.

June 20th.

I've been home a month. I've got tails to my dresses and silk linings, and my hair done up like the people in advertisements, and parasols with frills, and a pearl necklace to wear at nights with real evening dresses. I wear white veils, too, and such sweet hats—I don't mind saying it here where no one will see, but I really do look most awfully nice. I should just simply love to be lolling back in the victoria, all frills and feathers, and the crocodiles to march by. Wouldn't they stare! It was always so interesting to see how the girls looked grown up.

The weather has been lovely, and I do think ours is the very dearest old house in the world. It is described in the guide-books as "a fine old Jacobean mansion," and all sorts of foreign royal creatures have stayed here as a place of refuge in olden days before father's people bought it. It is red brick covered with ivy, and at the right side the walls go out in a great semicircle, with windows all round giving the most lovely view. Opposite the door is a beautiful old cedar, which I used to love to climb as a child, and should now if I had my own way. Its lower branches dip down to the grass and make the most lovely bridge to the old trunk. On the opposite side of the lawn there's another huge tree; hardly anyone knows what it is, but it's a Spanish maple really—such a lovely thing, all shining silver leaves on dark stems. I used to look from one to the other and think that they looked like youth and age, and summer and winter, and all sorts of poetical things like that.

On the south side there is another entrance leading down to the terrace by a long flight of stone stairs, the balustrades of which are covered by a tangle of clematis and roses. When I come walking down those steps and see the peacock strutting about in the park, and the old sundial, and the row of beeches in the distance, I feel a thrill of something that makes me hot and cold and proud and weepy all at the same time. Father says he feels just the same, in a man-ey way, of course, and that it is much the same thing as patriotism—love of the soil that has come down to you from generations of ancestors, and that it's a right and natural feeling and ought to be encouraged. I know it is in him, for he will deny himself anything and everything to keep the place in order and give his tenants a good time, but—Resolution number two—I, Una Sackville, solemnly vow to speak the plain truth about my own feelings in this book, and not cover them up with a cloak of fine words—I think there's a big sprinkling of conceit in my feelings. I *do* like being the Squire's daughter, and having people stare at me as I go through the town, and rush about to attend to me when I enter a shop. Ours is only a little bit of a town, and there is so little going on that people take an extra special interest in us and our doings. I know some of the girls quite well—the vicar's daughter and the doctor's, and the Heywood girls at the Grange, and I am always very nice to them, but I feel all the time that I am being nice, and they feel it too, so we never seem to be real friends. Is that being a snob, I wonder? If it is, it's as much their fault as mine, because they are quite different to me from what they are to each other—so much more polite and well-behaved.

I spend the mornings with father, and the afternoons with mother. At first she had mapped out my whole day for me—practising, reading, driving, etcetera, but I just said straight out that I'd promised to go the rounds with father, and I think she was glad, though very much surprised.

"He will be so pleased to have you! It's nice of you, dear, to think of it, and after all it will be exercise, and there's not much going on in the morning."

She never seemed to think I should enjoy it, and I suppose it would bore her as much to walk round to the stables and kennels, and talk to the keepers about game, and the steward about new roofs to cottages, and cutting timber, as it does him to go to garden-parties and pay formal calls. It seems strange to live together so long and to be so different.

I have not met many strangers as yet, because Vere is bringing down a party of visitors for August, and mother is not in a hurry to take me about until I have got all my things; but one morning, when I was out with father, I met such a big, handsome man, quite young, with a brown face and laughing eyes, dressed in the nice country fashion which I love—Norfolk jacket, knickerbockers and leggings. Father hailed him at once, and they talked together for a moment without taking any notice of me, and then father remembered me suddenly, and said—

"This is my youngest daughter. Come home from school to play with me, haven't you, Babs?" and the strange man smiled and nodded, and said, "How do, Babs?" just as calmly and patronisingly as if I had been two. For a moment I was furious, until I remembered my hockey skirt and cloth cap, and hair done in a door-knocker, with no doubt ends flying about all round my face. I daresay I looked fourteen at the most, and he thought I was home for the holidays. I decided that it would be rather fun to foster the delusion, and behave just as I liked without thinking of what was proper all the time, and then some day he would find out his mistake, and feel properly abashed. His name is Will Dudley, and he is staying with Mr Lloyd, the agent for the property which adjoins father's, learning how to look after land, for some day he will inherit a big estate from an uncle, so he likes to get all the experience he can, and to talk to father, and go about with him whenever he has the chance, and father likes to have him—I could tell it by the way he looks and talks. We walked miles that morning, over gates and stiles, and across brooks without dreaming of waiting for the bridges, and I climbed and splashed with the best, and Mr Dudley twinkled his eyes at me, and said, "Well jumped, Babs!" and lifted me down from the stiles as if I had been a doll. He must be terrifically strong, for I am no light weight, and he didn't seem to feel me at all.

After that morning we were constantly meeting, and we grew to be quite friends. He has thick, crinkly eyebrows, and is clean-shaven, which I like in his case, as his mouth has such a nice expression. He went on treating me as a child, and father seemed to think it was

13

quite natural. He likes to pretend I am young, poor dear, so that I may be his playmate as long as possible.

Yesterday father went in to see some cottagers, and Mr Dudley and I sat outside on a log of wood, and talked while we waited for him like this. He—patronisingly—

"I suppose it's a great treat for you to getaway from school for a time. Where is your school? Town or country? Brighton—ugh!" and he made a grimace of disgust. "Shops—piers—hotels—an awful place! Not a bit of Nature left unspoiled; the very sea looks artificial and unlike itself in such unnatural surroundings!"

"Plenty of crocodiles on the bank, however—that's natural enough!" I said pertly. I thought it was rather smart, too, but he smiled in a superior "I-will-because-I-must," sort of way, and said—

"How thankful you must be to get away from it all to this exquisite calm!"

I don't know much about young men, except what I've seen of Spencer and his friends, but they would call exquisite calm by a very different name, so I decided at once that Mr Will Dudley must have had a secret trouble which had made him hate the world and long for solitude. Perhaps it was a love affair! It would be interesting if he could confide in me, and I could comfort him, so I looked pensive, and said—

"You do get very tired of the glare and the dust! Some of the girls wear smoked glasses in summer, and you get so sick of marching up and down the front. Do you hate Brighton only, or every towny place?"

"I hate all towns, and can't understand how anyone can live in them who is not obliged. I have tried it for the last five years, but never again!" He stretched his big shoulders, and drew a long breath of determination. "I've said 'Good-bye' for ever to a life of trammelled civilisation, with its so-called amusements and artificial manners, and hollow friendships, and"—he put his hand to his flannel collar, and patted it with an air of blissful satisfaction—"and stiff, uncomfortable clothing! It's all over and done with now, thank goodness—a dream of the past!"

"And I am just beginning it! And I expect to like it very much," I thought to myself, but I didn't say so to him; and he went on muttering and grumbling all the time he was rolling his cigarette and preparing to smoke.

"You don't understand—a child like you. It's a pity you ever should, but in a few years' time you will be so bound round with conventions that you will not dare to follow your own wishes, unless you make a bold stroke for liberty, as I have done, and free yourself once for all; but not many people have the courage to do that—"

"I don't think it takes much courage to give up what one dislikes, and to do what one likes best," I said calmly; and he gave a little jump of surprise, and stared at me over the smoke of the match with amused eyes, just as you look at a child who has said a funny thing—rather precocious for its age.

"Pray, does that wise remark apply to me or to you?" he asked; and I put my chin in the air and said—

"It was a general statement. Of course, I can't judge of your actions, and, for myself, I can't tell as yet what I *do* like. I must try both lives before I can decide."

"Yes, yes. You must run the gauntlet. Poor little Babs!" he sighed; and after that we sat for quite an age without speaking a word. He was remembering his secret, no doubt, and I was thinking of myself and wondering if it was really true that I was going to have such a bad time. That reminded me of Miss Martin and her advice, and it came to me with a shock that I'd been home a whole month, and had been so taken up with my own affairs that I had had no time to think of my "sister." I was in a desperate hurry to find her at once. I always am in a hurry when I remember things, and the sight of the cottages put an idea into my head.

"Do you know the people who live in these cottages, Mr Dudley? I knew the old tenants, of course, but these are new people, and I have not seen them. Are they old or young, and have they any children?"

He puffed out words and smoke in turns.

"John Williams—*puff*—wife—*puff*—one baby, guaranteed to make as much noise as five—it's a marvel it's quiet now—*puff*. You can generally hear it a mile off—"

"Is it ill, then, the poor little thing?"

"Healthiest child in the world to judge from its appearance and the strength of its lungs! Natural depravity, nothing else"—*puff*!

"And in the next house?"

"Thompson—oldish man—widower. Maiden sister to keep the house in order—Thompson, too, I suspect by the look of him. Looks very sorry for himself, poor soul!"

"What's the matter with him—rheumatism? Is he quite crippled or able to get about?"

"Thompson? Splendid workman—agile as a boy. It was his mental condition to which I referred!"

"And in the end house of all?"

"Don't know the name. Middle-aged couple, singularly uninteresting, and two big hulking sons—"

Big—hulking! It was most disappointing! *No one* was delicate! I twisted about on my seat, and cried irritably—

"Are they *all* well, every one of them? Are you quite sure? Are there no invalid daughters, or crippled children, nor people like that?"

"Not that I know of, thank goodness! You don't mean to say you *want* them to be ill?" He stared at me as if I were mad, and then suddenly his face changed, and he said softly, "Oh, I see! You want to look after them! That's nice of you, and it would have been uncommonly nice for them, too; but, never fear, you will find plenty of people to help, if that's what you want. Their troubles may not take quite such an obvious form as crutches, but they are in just as much need of sympathy, nevertheless. In this immediate neighbourhood, for instance—" He paused for a moment, and I knew he was going to make fun by the twinkle in his eye and the solemn way he puffed out the smoke. "There's—myself!" So I just paid him back for his patronage, and led up to the mystery by saying straight out—

"Yes, I know! I guessed by what you said about town that you had had some disappointment. I'm dreadfully sorry, and if there's anything at all that I can do—"

He simply jumped with surprise and stared at me in dead silence for a moment, and then—horrid creature!—he began to laugh and chuckle as if it was the most amusing thing in the world.

"So you have been making up stories about me, eh? Am I a blighted creature? Am I hiding a broken heart beneath my Norfolk jacket? Has a lovely lady scorned me and left me in grief to pine—eh, Babs? I did not know you were harbouring such unkind thoughts of me. You can't accuse me of showing signs of melancholy this last week, I'm sure, and as to my remarks about town, they were founded on nothing more romantic than my rooted objection to smoke and dust, and bachelor diggings with careless landladies. I assure you I have no tragic secrets to disclose! I'm sorry, as I'm sure you would find me infinitely more interesting with a broken heart."

"Oh, I'm exceedingly glad, of course; but if you are so happy and contented I don't see how you need my help," I said disagreeably;

and just then father came out of the cottage, and we started for home.

Mr Dudley talked to him about business in the most proper fashion, but if he caught my eye, even in the middle of a sentence, he would drop his head on his chest and put on the most absurd expression of misery, and then I would toss my head and smile a scornful smile. Some day, when he finds out how old I am, he will be ashamed of treating me like a child.

William Dudley is the first stranger mentioned in these pages. For that reason I shall always feel a kind of interest in him, but I am disappointed in his character.

Chapter Four.

July 10th.

To-day I went a round of calls with mother, driving round the country for over twenty miles. It was rather dull in one way and interesting in another, for I do like to see other people's drawing-rooms and how they arrange the things. Some are all new and garish, and look as if they were never used except for an hour or two in the evening, and some are grand and stiff like a hotel, and others are all sweet and chintzy and home-like, with lots of plants and a scent of *pot-pourri* in china vases. That's the sort of room I like. I mean to marry a man who belongs to a very ancient family, so that I may have lots of beautiful old furniture.

Mother gave me histories of the various hostesses as we drove up to the houses.

"A dreadfully trying woman, I do hope she is out." "Rather amusing. I should like you to see her." "A most hopeless person—absolutely no conversation. Now, darling, take a lesson from her and never, never allow yourself to relapse into monosyllables. It is such a hopeless struggle if all one's remarks are greeted with a 'No' or a 'Yes,' and when girls first come out they are very apt to fall into this habit. Make a rule that you will never reply to a question in less than four words, and it is wonderful what a help you will find it.

"Twist the ends of your veil, dear, they are sticking out... Oh dear, dear, she is at home! I do have such shocking bad fortune."

She trailed out of the carriage sighing so deeply that I was terrified lest the servant should hear. I shall never call on people unless I want to see them. It does seem such a farce to grumble because they are at home, and then to be sweet and pleasant when you meet.

Mrs Greaves was certainly very silent, but I liked her. She looked worn and tired, but she had beautiful soft brown eyes which looked at you and seemed to say a great deal more than her lips. Do you know the kind of feeling when you like people and know they like you in return? I was perfectly certain Mrs Greaves had taken a fancy to me before she said, "I should like to introduce my daughter to you," and sent a message upstairs by the servant. I wondered what the girl would be like; a young edition of Mrs Greaves might be pretty, but there was an expression on mother's face which made me uncertain. Then she came in, a pale badly dressed girl, with a sweet face and shy awkward manners. Her name was Rachel, and she took me to see the conservatory, and I wondered what on earth we should find to say. Of course she asked first of all —

"Are you fond of flowers?" and I remembered mother's rule and replied, "Yes, I love them." That was four words, but it didn't seem to take us much further somehow, so I made a terrific effort and added, "But I don't know much about their names, do you?"

"Yes, I think I do. I feel as if it was a kind of courtesy we owe them for giving us so much pleasure. We take it as a slight if our own friends mispronounce or misspell our own names, and surely flowers deserve as much consideration from us," quoth she.

Goodness! how frightfully proper and correct. I felt so quelled that there was no more spirit left in me, and I followed her round listening to her learned descriptions and saying, "How pretty!" "Oh, really!" in the most feeble manner you can imagine.

All the while I was really looking at her more than the flowers, and discovering lots of things. Number one—sweet eyes just like her mother's; number two—sweet lips with tiny little white teeth like a child's; number three—a long white throat above that awful collar. Quotient—a girl who ought to be quite sweet, but who made herself a fright. I wondered why! Did she think it wrong to look nice—but then, if she did, why did she love the flowers just for that very reason? Rachel Greaves! I thought the name sounded like her somehow—old-fashioned, and prim, and grey; but the next moment I felt ashamed, for, as if she guessed what I was thinking, she turned to me and said suddenly—

"Will you tell me your name? I ought to know it to add to my collection, for you are like a flower yourself."

Wasn't it a pretty compliment? I blushed like anything, and said —

"It must be a wild one, I'm afraid. I look hot-housey this afternoon, for I'm dressed up to pay calls, but really I have just left school, and feel as wild as I can be. You mustn't be shocked if you meet me in a short frock some morning tearing about the fields."

She leant back against the stand, staring at me with such big eyes, and then she said the very last thing in the world which I expected to hear.

"May I come with you? Will you let me come too some day?"

Come with me! Rachel Greaves, with her solemn face, and dragged-back hair, and her proper conversation. To tear about the fields! I nearly had a fit.

"I suppose you want to botanise?" I asked feebly, and she shook her head and said —

"No; I want to talk to you — I want to do just what you do when you are alone."

"Scramble through the hedges, and jump the streams, and swing on the gates, and go bird's-nesting in the hedges?"

She gave a gulp of dismay, but stuck to her guns.

"Y—es! At least, I could try — you could teach me. I've learned such a number of things in my life, but I don't know how to play. That part of my education has been neglected."

"Wherever did you go to school? What a dreadful place it must have been!"

"I never went to school; I had governesses at home, and I have no brothers nor sisters; I am very much interested in girls of my own age, especially poor girls, and try to work among them, but I am not very successful. They are afraid of me, and I can't enter into their amusements; but if I could learn to romp and be lively, it might be different."

It was such a funny thing to ask, and she looked so terribly in earnest over it, that I was simply obliged to laugh.

"Do you mean to say you want to learn to be lively, as a lesson—that you are taking it up like wood-carving or poker-work—for the sake of your class and your influence there?"

She blinked at me like an owl, and said—

"I think, so far as I can judge of my own motives, that that is a truthful statement of the case! I have often wished I knew someone like you—full of life and spirit; but there are not many girls in this neighbourhood, and I met no one suitable until you came. It is a great deal to ask, but if you would spend a little time with me sometimes I should be infinitely grateful."

"Oh, don't be grateful, please, until you realise what you have to endure. Nothing worth having can be gained without suffering," I said solemnly. "I shall lead you a terrible dance, and you must promise implicit obedience. I'm a terrible bully when I get the chance."

I privately determined that I'd teach her other things besides play, and we agreed to meet next morning at eleven o'clock to take our first walk. Mother was much amused when I told her of our conversation.

"You'll soon grow tired of her, darling; she is impossibly dull, but a good creature who can do you no harm. You can easily drop her if she bores you too much."

But I don't expect to be bored, I expect it will be very amusing.

Next Day.

It was! She was there to meet me with a mushroom hat over her face, looking as solemn as ever, and never in all my life did I see a poor creature work so hard at trying to enjoy herself. She runs like an elephant, and puffs like a grampus; says, "One, two, three," at the edge of the streams, then gives a convulsive leap, and lands right in the middle of the water. She was splashed from head to foot, and quite pink in the cheeks imagining she was going to be drowned, and in the next hedge her hat caught in a branch, and was literally torn from her head. Then we sat down to consider the situation, and to collect the fallen hairpins from the ground.

She has a great long rope of hair, and she twists and twists and twists it together like a nurse wringing out a fomentation, so I politely offered to fasten it for her, and loosened it out and pulled it up over her forehead, and you wouldn't believe the difference it made. We found some wild strawberries, and ate them for lunch, and I wreathed the leaves round her head, and when her fingers were nicely stained with the juice, and she looked thoroughly disreputable, I held out the little looking-glass on my chatelaine, and gave her a peep at herself, and said—

"That's the result of the first lesson! What do you think of the effect on your appearance?"

"I beg your pardon! I'm quite ashamed. What have I been doing?" she cried all in a breath, and up went both hands to drag her hair back, and tear out the leaves, but I caught them in time and held them down.

"Implicit obedience, remember! I like you better as you are. It's such pretty hair that it's a sin to hide it away in that tight little knot. Why shouldn't you look nice if you can?"

That began it, and we had quite a solemn discussion, something like this—

Rachel, solemnly: "It does not matter how we look, so long as our characters are beautiful!"

Una: "Then why was everything on the earth made so beautiful if we were not intended to be beautiful too? How would you like it if everything was just as useful, but looked ugly instead of pretty? When you have the choice of being one or the other it's very ungrateful to abuse your talent!"

"Beauty a talent! I have always looked upon it as a snare! How many a woman's life has been spoiled by a lovely face!"

"That's the abuse of beauty, not the use!" I said, and felt quite proud of myself, for it sounded so grand. "Of course, if you were silly and conceited, it would spoil everything; but if you were nice, you would have far more influence with people. I used to notice that with the pretty girls at school, and, of course, there's mother—everyone adores her, and feels repaid for any amount of trouble if she will just smile and look pleased."

"Ah, your mother! But there are not many like her. You spoke of having a choice, but in my own case, for instance, how could I— what could I do?"

"You could look fifty thousand times nicer if you took the trouble. I thought so the first time I saw you, and now I know it. Look in the glass again; would you know yourself for the same girl?"

She peered at herself, and gave a pleased little smirk just like a human being.

"It's the enjoyment lesson, and the red cheeks—but oh, I couldn't—I really couldn't wear my hair like that! It looks so terribly as if I—I *wanted* to look nice!"

"Well, so you do, don't you? I do, frightfully! I'd like to be perfectly lovely, and so charming that everyone adored me, and longed to be with me."

"Ah, that's different," she said softly, and her eyes went shiny and she stared straight ahead at nothing, in the way people do who are thinking nice thoughts of their own which they don't mean you to know. "To be loved is beautiful, but that is different from admiration. We love people for their gifts of mind and heart, not for their appearance." She meandered on for quite a long time, but I really forget all she said, for I was getting tired of moralising, and wondering what excuse I could make to leave her and fly off home across the fields. Then suddenly came the sound of footsteps at the other side of the stile, and who should come jumping over just before our very faces but Will Dudley himself on his way home to lunch. He stared for a moment, hardly recognising the two hat-less, dishevelled mortals squatted on the grass, and then came forward to shake hands. The funny thing was that he came to me first, and said, "How do you do?" and then just shook hands with Rachel without ever saying a word. She didn't say anything either, but I could see she was horribly embarrassed, thinking of her hair and the strawberry leaves, and he looked at her and looked again as if he could not understand what had happened.

I thought it would be fun to tell him all about it when we reached the cross-roads, and Rachel left us alone. I was glad she was going another way, because it's rather a nuisance having a stranger with you when you want to talk, and I knew Mr Dudley very well by this time. He would be so amused at the idea of the enjoyment lesson. I was looking forward to our talk; but oh, dear, what horrid shocks one does get sometimes! I shall never, never forget my feelings when we got to the corner, and he held out his hand to me—me—Una Sackville, and walked calmly off with Rachel Greaves.

It was not as if he had been going in her direction; his way home was with me, so why on earth should he choose to go off with her? Are they lovers, or friends, or what? Why did he take no notice of her at first, then suddenly become so anxious for her society? It's not that I care a scrap, but it seemed so rude! I've been as cross as two sticks all day. Nothing annoys me more than to be disappointed in my friends!

Eleven o'clock. I was comfortably settled in bed when I suddenly remembered resolution number two. The real reason that I am annoyed is that I am conceited enough to think I am nicer than Rachel, and to want Mr Dudley to think so too. How horrid it looks written down! I believe it will do me heaps of good to have to look at plain truths about myself in staring black and white. Perhaps Lorna is right after all, and I have a greed for admiration! I'll turn over a new leaf and be humble from this day.

Chapter Five.

July 15th.

I was not in the least interested to know anything about what Will Dudley and Rachel Greaves talked about together, but I was anxious to find out if she had said anything to show him that I was really grown-up, instead of the child he thought me; so the next time we met I asked her plump and plain—

"What did you and Mr Dudley say about me the other morning?"

We were walking along a lane together, and she turned her head and stared at me in blank surprise.

"About you? The other morning? We—we never spoke of you at all!"

Then I suppose I looked angry, or red, or something, for she seemed in a tremendous hurry to appease me.

"We have a great many interests in common. When we lived in town we belonged to the same societies, and worked for the same charities. It is interesting to remember old days, and tell each other the latest news we have heard about the work and its progress."

"Then you knew him before he came here? He is not a new friend?"

"Oh, no—we have known him for years. It was father who got him his present position."

"And you like him very much?"

"Yes," she said quietly. "Isn't it lovely to see the hedges covered with the wild roses? I think they are almost my favourite flower—so dainty and delicate."

"Nasty, prickly things—I hate them!" I cried; for I do detest being snubbed, and she could not have told me more plainly in so many words that she did not choose to speak of Will Dudley. Why not? I wonder. Was there some mystery about their friendship? I should not mind talking about anyone I know, and it was really absurd of Rachel to be so silent and reserved. I determined not to ask her any more questions, but to tackle Mr Dudley himself.

Two days after there was the garden party, where I knew we should meet. He was bound to go, as it was on the estate where he was living, and I was to make my first formal appearance in society, in the prettiest dress and hat you can possibly imagine. Mother was quite pleased with me because I let her and Johnson fuss as much as they liked, and tie on my white veil three times over to get it in the right folds. Then I looked in the glass at my sweeping skirts, and hair all beautifully done up, and laughed to think how different I looked from Babs of the morning hours.

We drove off in state, and I was quite excited at the prospect of the fray; but I do think garden parties are dreadfully dull affairs! A band plays on the lawn, and people stroll about, and criticise one another's dresses, and look at the flowers. They are very greedy affairs, too, for really and truly we were eating all the time—tea and iced coffee when we arrived; ices, and fruits, and nice things to drink until the moment we came away. I don't mean to say that I ate straight on, of course, but waiters kept walking about with trays, and I noticed particularly what they were like, so as not to take two ices running from the same man. I had a strawberry, and a vanilla, and a lemon—but that was watery, and I didn't like it. I was talking to the hostess, when I saw Mr Dudley coming towards us, and he looked at me with such a blank, unrecognising stare that I saw at once he had no idea who I was. Mrs Darcy talked to him for a moment while I kept the brim of my hat tilted over my face, then she said—

"Don't you know Miss Sackville? Allow me to introduce Mr Dudley, dear. Do take her to have some refreshment, like a good man. I am sure she has had nothing to eat!"

I thought of the coffee, and the ices, and the lemonade and the sandwiches, but said nothing, and we sauntered across the lawn together talking in the usual ridiculous grown-up fashion.

"Lovely day, isn't it?"

"Quite charming. So fortunate for Mrs Darcy."

"Beautiful garden, isn't it?"

"Charming! Such lovely roses!"

"Beautiful band, isn't it?"

"Oh, charming! Quite charming!"

Then he seated me at a little table and provided me with an ice, (number four), and stared furtively at me from the opposite side. It *was* fun. I crinkled my veil up over my nose and tilted my hat over my forehead, and shot a glance at him every now and then, to find his eyes fixed on me—not recognising at all, but evidently so puzzled and mystified to think who I could be. Father had told him only a week before that Vere would not be home for a month—and now who was this third Miss Sackville who had suddenly appeared upon the scene?

"You have returned home rather sooner than you intended, haven't you?" he inquired, and I shook my head and said—

"Oh, no, I kept to the exact date. I always do! What makes you think otherwise?"

"I—er—I thought I heard you were not expected for some time to come. You have been staying with friends?"

"Oh, a number of friends! Quite a huge house party. I feel quite lost without them all."

He would have been rather surprised if I had explained that the party consisted of forty women and no man, but that was not his business, and it was perfectly true that I missed them badly. All the Rachel Greaveses in the world would never make up for Lorna and the rest!

"But you have your sister!" he said. "I have seen a good deal of your sister in her morning walks with Mr Sackville. She is a charming child, and most companionable; I am sure she will be a host in herself!"

"It's very good of you! I can't tell you how pleased I am to hear you say so!" I said suavely; but do what I would, I could not resist a giggle, and he stared at me harder than ever, and looked so confused. I was so afraid that he would find me out and spoil the fun that I determined not to try to keep up the delusion any longer. He was going to cross-question me, I could see it quite plainly, so I lay back in my chair, smoothed out my veil, and smiled at him in my most fascinating manner.

"I'm so pleased that you have formed such a good opinion of me, Mr Dudley! I was really afraid you had forgotten me altogether, for you seemed hardly to recognise me a few minutes ago."

He leant both arms on the table so that his face was quite near to mine. "*Who are you?*" he asked, and I laughed, and nodded in reply.

"I'm Babs—Una Sackville is my name—England is my nation, Branfield is my dwelling—"

"Don't joke, please. I want to understand. *You—are—Babs*! Have you been deliberately deceiving me, then? Pray, what has been your object in posing as a child all these weeks!"

That made me furious, and I cried hotly—

"I never posed at all—I never deceived you! Father treats me as a child, and you followed his example as a matter of course, and I was very pleased to be friends in a sensible manner without any nonsense. If I had said, 'Please, I'm nineteen—I've left school, and am coming out—this is a hockey skirt, but I wear tails in the evening,' you would have been proper, and stiff, and have talked about the weather, and we should have had no fun. If anyone is to blame, it is you, for not seeing how really old I was!"

He smiled at that, and went on staring, staring at my face, my hair, my long white gloves, the muslin flounces lying on the ground round my feet.

"So very old!" he said. "Nineteen, is it? And I put you down as— fourteen or fifteen, at the most! And so Babs has disappeared. Exit Babs! I'm sorry. She was a nice child; I enjoyed meeting her very much. I think we should have been real good friends."

"She has not disappeared at all. You will meet her to-morrow morning. There is nothing to prevent us being as good friends as ever," I declared, but he shook his head in a mysterious fashion.

"I think there is! There's a third person on the scene now who will make it difficult—for me, at least—to go back to the same footing. There's Una!" he said, and looked at me with his bright grey eyes, up and down, down and up again, in a grave, quiet sort of way which I had never seen before. It made me feel nice, but rather uncomfortable, and I was glad when he brightened up again, and said gaily—

"I owe a hundred apologies for my lack of ceremony to this fine, this very fine, this super-fine young lady! I'll turn over a new leaf for the future, and treat you with becoming ceremony. I can quite imagine the disgust of the budding *débutante* at my cavalier ways. Confess now that your dignity was sorely wounded?"

His eyes were twinkling again. They are grey, and his face is so brown that they look lighter than the skin. I never saw anyone's eyes look like that before, but it is awfully nice. I thought there was a splendid opening, so I said—

"No; I was never vexed but once. I like being treated sensibly, but that morning when you left me, and went out of your way with Rachel Greaves—I was sorry then that you did not know that I was grown up."

"You thought if I had I would have walked with you instead? Why?"

I blushed a little, and it seemed to me that he blushed too—his cheeks certainly looked hot. It was a horrid question to answer, and he must have known for himself what I meant. I really and truly don't think many men would go out of their way for Rachel Greaves. I answered by another question—it was the easiest way.

"I didn't know then that you were old friends. I suppose you get to like her better when you know her well?"

"Naturally. That is always the case with the best people."

"And she is—"

"The best woman I have ever met, and the most selfless!" he said solemnly. "Have you spoken to Rachel about me? What has she told you? I should like you to know the truth, though it is not yet general property. You can keep it to yourself for awhile?"

I nodded. I didn't want to speak, for I felt a big, hard lump swelling in my throat, and my heart thumped. I knew quite well what he was going to say, and I hated it beforehand.

"We are engaged to be married. It will probably be an engagement for years, for Rachel feels her present duty is at home, and I am content to wait her pleasure. I don't go up to the house very often, as the old gentleman is an invalid, and dislikes visitors, but we understand one another, and are too sensible to fret because we cannot always be together. Only when an opportunity occurs, as it did the other morning— Why—you understand?"

"Yes, I understand," I said slowly. I was thinking it over, and wondering, if I were ever engaged, if I should like my *fiancé* to be content and sensible, and quite resigned to see me seldom, and to wait for years before we could be married. I think I would rather he were in a hurry!

Oh, I wish I were selfless, too! I wish I could be glad for them without thinking of myself; but I do feel so lonely and out in the cold. I'm thankful that Vere is coming home next week, and the house will be filled with visitors. Engaged people are no use—they are always thinking about each other!

Chapter Six.

July 20th.

Rachel was surprised when I told her that I knew her secret, and I don't think she was pleased.

"Will told you! Will told you himself!" she repeated, and stared at me in a puzzled, curious fashion, as if she wondered why on earth he should have chosen to make a confidante of me. "It is hardly a regular engagement, for father will not hear of my leaving home, and the waiting may be so long that I have told Will it is not fair to bind him. He says he is content to wait, but we agreed to speak about it as little as possible for some time to come."

"Oh, well, I'll keep the secret. You need not be afraid that I shall gossip about you," I told her. She wears no ring on her engagement finger, but always, always—morning, noon and night—there is a little diamond anchor pinned in the front of her dress. I suppose he has given her that instead, as a symbol of hope—hope that in ten or a dozen years, when she is an old thing over thirty, they may possibly be married! Well, I can imagine Rachel waiting twenty years, if it comes to that, and keeping quite happy and serene meantime; but Will Dudley is different—so quick and energetic and keen. I could not have imagined him so patient.

Yesterday Vere came home, bringing her friends with her, and already Rachel and her love affair seems far away, and we live in such a bustle and confusion that there is no time to think. I'm rather glad, for I was getting quite dull and mopey. They arrived about five in the afternoon, and came trooping into the hall, where tea was waiting. Two girls and three men, and Vere herself, prettier than ever, but with just the old, aggravating, condescending way.

"Hallo, Babs! Is that you transformed into a young lady in long dresses, and your hair done up? You dear, fat thing, how ridiculous you look!" she cried, holding me out at arm's length, and laughing as if it were the funniest joke in the world, while those three strange men stood by staring, and I grew magenta with embarrassment.

One of the men was tall and handsome, with a long, narrow face, and small, narrow eyes; he laughed with her, and I hated him for it, and for having so little sympathy with a poor girl's feelings. Another was small, with a strong, square-set figure, and he looked sorry for me; and the third looked on the floor, and frowned as if something had hurt his feelings. He was the oldest and gravest-looking of the three, and I knew before he had been ten minutes in the room that he adored Vere with his heart, and disapproved of her with his conscience, and was miserable every time she did or said a thoughtless thing.

"I told you I had a smaller sister at home—here she is! Rather bigger than I expected, but not much changed in other respects. Don't be shy, Babs! Shake hands nicely, and be friends!" Vere cried laughingly, taking me by the shoulders and pushing me gently towards where the men stood; but, just as I was fuming with rage at being treated as if I were two, father came suddenly from behind, and said in his most grand seigneur manner—

"Allow me, Vere! If an introduction is made at all, it is best to make it properly. Captain Grantly, Mr Nash, Mr Carstairs, I have the honour of introducing you to my second daughter, Miss Una Sackville."

The change of expression on the men's faces was comical to behold. Captain Grantly, the narrow-faced one, bowed as if I had been the Queen, and the nice little man smiled at me as if he were pleased—he was Mr Nash, and poor Mr Carstairs flushed as if he had been snubbed himself; I was quite sorry for him.

The girls were very lively and bright, spoke in loud voices, and behaved as if they had lived in the house all their lives, which is supposed to be good manners nowadays. Margot Sanders is tall and fair, and wears eye-glasses, and Mary Eversley, who is "Lady Mary," would have been considered very unladylike indeed at our polite seminary.

It seems to be fashionable nowadays for a girl to behave as much like a man as possible, and to smoke and shout, and stand with her arms behind her back, and lounge about anyhow on her chair. Well, I won't! I don't care if it's fashionable or not! I'd rather have been a boy if I'd had the choice, but as I am a girl I'll make the best of it, and be as nice a specimen as I can. Lorna says a girl ought to be like a flower—sweet, modest and fragrant; she's a bit sentimental when you get her alone, but I agree with the idea, though I should not have expressed it in the same way. If I were a man I should hate to marry a girl who smelt of tobacco and shrieked like a steam whistle. I'd like a dear, dainty thing with a soft voice and pretty, womanly ways. I hereby vow and declare that I will stick to my colours, and set an example to those old things who ought to know better. Lady Mary must be twenty-five if she is a day. I don't expect she will ever be married now. With the clear-sighted gaze of youth, I can see that she is hiding a broken heart beneath the mask of mirth. Life is frightfully exciting when you have the gift of penetrating below the surface.

Will Dudley came to dinner; he was the only stranger, as he made the number even. I wore my new white chiffon, and thought I looked very fine till I went downstairs and saw the others. They were smart, and Vere looked lovely, and did the honours so charmingly that even mother seemed to make way for her. Poor mother! she looked so happy; she dotes on Vere, and is so proud of her; it does seem hard she doesn't have more of her society! I felt sad somehow, and sort of lonely as I watched them together—Vere fussing round and saying pretty, flattering little speeches, and mother smiling at her so tenderly. I feel nice things, too, but I can't say them to order; my lips seem all tight and horrid, as if they wouldn't move. I felt like the elder brother in the parable, because I really have denied myself, and been bored fearfully sometimes these last weeks doing fancy-work with mother, and driving about shut up in a horrid, close carriage, while Vere has been gadding about and enjoying herself; and then the moment she comes home I am nowhere beside her! Injustices like this sear the heart, and make one old before one's time.

I suppose I looked sad, for Will Dudley crossed over the room to talk to me.

"Aren't you well?" he asked, and his eyes looked so anxious and worried that it quite comforted me.

"I have rather a headache," I began, without thinking of what I was saying, and then, (somehow I never can help telling him exactly how I feel), I stopped, and contradicted myself flat. "I'm perfectly well, but I think I'm jealous. I have been the only child for so long, and now my poor little nose is out of joint, and I don't like it a bit. It aches."

I thought he would sympathise and protest that I could never be superseded, in his opinion at least, but he just sighed, and said slowly—

"Yes, she is very lovely! It must be a great responsibility to have a face as beautiful as hers, with all the influence over others that is its accompaniment!" and looked straight across the room to where Vere stood beneath the shaded lamp.

She was not looking in our direction; but, as if she felt his gaze without seeing it, she turned her head slowly round and raised her eyes to his, and so they stood while you could have counted ten, staring, staring, straight into each other's eyes, and I saw the colour fade gradually out of Vere's face as though she were frightened by what she saw. That is the way people fall in love! I've read about it in books. They sort of recognise each other when they meet, even if they are perfect strangers, and Lorna says it is the soul recognising its mate. But I know well enough that Vere would never satisfy Will Dudley, and, besides, there is Rachel—poor patient Rachel, who trusts him so faithfully. I looked up quickly to see if he had turned pale also. He was rather white, but there was a curious little smile about the corners of his lips which quietened my fears. I should not have liked that smile if I had been Vere. There was something contemptuous in it despite its admiration, and a sort of defiance, too, as if he were quite, quite sure of himself and secure from all temptation; but then they do begin like that sometimes, and the siren weaves on them her spells, and they succumb. I wonder how it will end with Vere and Will Dudley!

Chapter Seven.

It is rather jolly having a house full of people; and father and mother and Vere are so clever at entertaining. There is never any fuss nor effort, and people are allowed to go their own way, but there is always something to do if they choose to do it. I must say that, for grown-up people, these visitors are very frivolous, and play about together as if they were children. Mr Nash began showing me tricks with pennies after breakfast the first morning, and I was so interested learning how to do them that it was half-past ten before I thought of joining father at the stables. It was too late then, and I wasn't altogether sorry, for it was livelier going about with these new people, and it wasn't my fault, for I should have gone if I'd remembered. I was extra nice to father at lunch to make up, and he didn't seem a bit vexed, so I needn't trouble another day. Really, I think it is my duty to help Vere all I can. She questioned me about Will Dudley the first time we were alone. I knew she would, and decided to tell her of his engagement. I had been told not to speak of it generally; but to my own sister it was different, and I had a feeling that she ought to know.

"Who is that Mr Dudley?" she asked, and when I told her all I knew, she smiled and dropped her eyes in the slow, self-confident fashion which other people think so fascinating but which always make me long to shake her.

"Really, quite an acquisition!" she drawled. "A vast improvement on the native one generally meets in these wilds. We must cultivate him, Babs! He makes our number even, so we can afford to spoil him a little bit, as it is a convenience to ourselves at the same time. It will be a godsend for him to meet some decent people."

"As a matter of fact, he came to live in the country because he was sick of society and society people. He is not a country bumpkin, Vere, and won't be a bit grateful for your patronage. In fact, I don't believe he will come oftener than once or twice. When a man is engaged it's a bore to him to have to—"

"Engaged!" she cried. "Mr Dudley! Who told you he was engaged? I don't believe a word of it. Some stupid local gossip! Who told you that nonsense?"

"He told me himself!"

"He did? My dear Babs, he was having a joke! No man would confide such a thing to a child like you!"

"You are mistaken there. He has told me heaps of things besides this, and I know the girl, and have spoken to her about it. You know her, too. Rachel Greaves, who lives at 'The Clift'."

"Rach—el Greaves! Oh! oh!" cried Vere, and put her hands to her sides in peals of derisive laughter. "Oh, this is too killing! And you *believed* it? You dear, sweet innocent! That man and—Rachel Greaves! My dear, have you seen her hair? Have you seen her hat? Could you really imagine for one moment that any man could be engaged to a creature like that?"

"I don't imagine—I know! They have been engaged for years. It will be years more before they are married, for old Mr Greaves won't give his consent. And Rachel won't leave home without it; but Mr Dudley is quite willing to wait. He says she is the best woman in the world."

"Oh, I daresay! She is frumpy enough for anything; and you call that an engagement? My dear, he will no more marry her than he'll marry the moon. It's just a stupid platonic friendship, and as he has not known anything else he thinks it is love. Imagine being in love with that solemn creature! Imagine making pretty speeches and listening to her correct copy-book replies! Wait! I should think she may wait! She'll have a surprise one of these days when he meets the right girl, and bids Rachel Greaves a fond farewell!"

"He'll do nothing of the sort," I said hotly. "I do hate you, Vere, when you sneer like that, and make out that everyone is worldly and horrible, like yourself! Will Dudley is a good man, and he wants a good woman for his wife—not a doll. He'd rather have Rachel's little finger than a dozen empty-headed fashion-plates like the girls you admire. But you don't understand. Your friends are all so different that you cannot understand an honest man when you meet him."

"Can't I? What a pity! Don't get into a rage, dear, it's so unnecessary. I'm sorry I'm so obtuse; but at least I can learn. I'll make it my business to understand Mr Dudley thoroughly during the autumn. It will be quite an occupation," replied Vere, with her head in the air and her eyes glittering at me in a nasty, horrid, cold, calculating "You-wait-and-see" kind of way which made me ill! It was just like Tennyson's Lady Clara Vere de Vere, who "sought to break a country heart for pastime ere she went to town," for Vere would never be content to marry Will Dudley, even if she succeeded in winning him from Rachel. Poor Rachel! I felt so sorry for her; she has so little, and she's so sweet and content, and so innocent that a serpent has entered into her Eden. It sounds rather horrid to call your own sister a serpent, but circumstances alter cases, and it really is appropriate. I think Vere expected me to fly into another rage, but I didn't feel angry at all, only sorry and ashamed, and anxious to know what I could do to baulk her dark designs.

"I'm thankful I'm not a beauty!" I said at last, and she stared for a moment, and then laughed and said—

"Because of the terrible temptations which you escape? Dear little innocent! Don't be too modest, however; you really have improved marvellously these past few months. If you could hear what the men said about you last night—"

"I don't want to hear, thank you," I returned icily; and that was one temptation overcome, anyhow, for I just died to know every single remark! It's awful to care so much about what people think about you, as I do. After she went away I sat down and reviewed the situation, as they say in books, and mapped out a plan of action. I wanted to feel that I was doing some good to someone, so I decided then and there to be a guardian angel to Will and Rachel. It's wonderful what you can do, even if you are only nineteen and a girl, if you set your mind to it, and determine to succeed. They have both been kind to me, and I am their friend, and mean to help them. I'd rather be flayed alive than say so to a living soul, but I can now confess to these pages that I was jealous of Rachel myself when I first heard of the engagement, and I wondered, if Will had never seen her, if perhaps he—oh, a lot of silly, idiotic things; for he is so different from the other men you meet that you simply can't help liking him. So now it will be a discipline for me to have to forget myself, and try to keep them together. Perhaps when they are married they will know all, and bless my memory, and call one of their children after me, and I shall be content to witness their happiness from afar. I've read of things like that, but I always thought I'd be the married one, not the other. You do when you are young, but it's awful what sorrows there are in the world. I am not twenty yet, and already my life is blighted, and my fondest hopes laid in the dust...

Such ripping fun! We are all going for a moonlight party up the river, with hampers full of good things to eat at supper on the bank above the lock. We are taking rugs to spread on the grass, and Japanese lanterns to make it look festive, and not a single servant, so that we shall do everything ourselves. We girls are all delighted, but I think the men—Captain Grantly especially—think it's rather mad to go to so much trouble when you might have your dinner comfortably at home. Male creatures are like that, so practical and commonplace, not a bit enthusiastic and sensible like school-girls. We used to keep awake until one o'clock in the morning, and sit shivering in dressing-gowns, eating custard, tarts and sardines, and thought it was splendid fun. I think a picnic where servants make the fire and pack away the dishes is too contemptible for words.

Vere wanted Will Dudley to come with us, so I went round to the "The Clift" that very afternoon and invited Rachel to come too. I am as much at liberty to invite my friends as she is to ask hers, and this was meant to be a checkmate to her plans; but Rachel was too stupid for words, and wouldn't be induced to accept.

"I always play a game with father in the evening," she said. "He would miss it if I went out."

"But he can't expect you never to go out! He would appreciate you all the more if you did leave him alone sometimes," I said, talking to myself as much as to her, for it was four days since I had been a walk with my father, and my horrid old conscience was beginning to prick. "Do come, Rachel. I want you particularly," but she went on refusing, so then I thought I would try what jealousy would do. "We shall be such a merry party; Vere is prettier and livelier than ever, and her friends are very amusing. Lady Mary is very handsome, and she sings and plays on the mandoline. She is going to take it with her to-night. It will be so pretty, the sound of singing on the water, and she will look so picturesque under the Japanese lamps."

She looked wistful and longing, but not a bit perturbed.

"I wish I could come! It sounds charming. I've hardly ever been on the river, never in the evening; but I should be worrying about father all the time. He is old, you see, Una, and he has such bad pain, and his days seem so long. It must be so sad to be ill and know that you will never get any better, and to have nothing to look forward to." Her face lit up suddenly, and I knew she was thinking of the time, years ahead, when what she was looking forward to would come true. "I really could not neglect father for my own amusement."

"But you have someone else to think of!" I reminded her cunningly. "I told you who was coming. You ought to think of his pleasure."

"Oh, he will enjoy it in any case! He loves being on the water; I am so glad you asked him!" she cried, quite flushed with delight, if you please, at the thought that Will was coming without her. I did feel a worm! Never, no, never could I be like that. If I were engaged to a man and couldn't go anywhere, I should like him to stay at home too, and think of me, and not dare to enjoy himself with other girls; but Rachel is not like that. Sometimes I wish she were just a wee, tiny bit less sensible and composed. I could love her better if she were.

We all went down to the boat-house at eight o'clock, we girls with long coats over our light dresses, because it's silly to catch cold, and so unbecoming, and on the way I told Will about Rachel. He came at once and walked beside me, and gave me such a nice look as he thanked me for thinking of it.

"That was kind of you! She would be pleased to be remembered, but this sort of thing is out of her line. She will be happier at home!"

Poor Rachel! That's the worst of being chronically unselfish; in the end people cease to give you any credit for it, and virtue has to be its own reward, for you don't get any other. I did think it was hard that even Will should misjudge her so, and be so complacent about it into the bargain, but it was hardly my place to defend her to him, of all people in the world.

"You will come into my boat, of course," he said in his masterful way when we drew near the ferry; but I had seen Vere divide parties before now, and I knew very well I should not be allowed to go where I chose. It was as good as a play to see how she did it, seeming to ponder and consider, and change her mind half a dozen times, and to be so spontaneous and natural, when all the time her plans had been made from the very beginning. Finally, she and Will took possession of the first boat, with Lady Mary and Captain Grantly, who were always together, and were too much taken up with their own society to have eyes for anyone else. Miss Talbot, Mr Nash, Mr Carstairs and I went into the second boat—Miss Talbot furious because she felt it a slight to be put with a child like me—Mr Carstairs depressed as he generally was, poor man!—I with a heavy weight inside me, feeling all of a sudden as if I hated parties and everything about them, and dear little Mr Nash, happy and complacent, cracking jokes to which no one deigned to listen. Isn't it funny to think how miserable you can be when you are supposed to be enjoying yourself? I dare say if you only knew it, lots of people have aching hearts when you envy them for being so happy. The people on the banks looked longingly at us, but three out of the four in our boat were as cross and dissatisfied as they could be; and it made it worse to hear them enjoying themselves in the other boat;

Vere's trills of laughter, and Lady Mary's gentlemanly "Ha, ha!" ringing out in response to the murmur of the men's voices. When you are on land with the wrong people there is always the chance of a change, but you *do* feel so "fixed" in a boat! I simply longed to reach the lock, and felt as cross as two sticks, until suddenly I met Mr Carstairs' eyes, looking, oh, so sad and hopeless, and I felt so sorry that I simply had to rouse up to cheer him. He must know perfectly well that Vere doesn't care for him, but he seems as if he could not help caring for her, and staying on and on, though he is miserable all the time, I like him! He has a good look in his face, and talks sensibly about interesting things, instead of everlastingly chaffing or paying compliments, which seems to be the fashion nowadays. I think I shall favour his suit, and try to help him.

I talked, and he looked first bored, and then amused, and in the end quite interested and happy, so that we drew up by the bank to join the others in quite a cheerful mood, much to my relief. It is humiliating to look left out in the cold, however much you may feel it.

Vere was flushed, and unlike herself somehow. She fussed over the laying out of the supper, and it wasn't like Vere to fuss, and whenever she wanted anything done she always turned first of all to Will Dudley, and half the time he was looking the other way and never noticed what she ask, when poor Mr Carstairs did it at once and got snubbed for his pains.

I was the youngest, and had to do all the uninteresting things, such as unpacking the spoons and forks, and taking the paper wrappings off the tumblers, while the others laid out the provisions and quarrelled over the best arrangement. But it was fun when we all sat down and began to eat. The Japanese lanterns were tied to the trees overhead, and made everything look bright and cheery, for the moon had hidden itself behind the clouds, and it had been just a wee bit cheerless the last half-hour. We heated the soup over a little spirit-lamp, and had lobster salad on dainty little paper plates, and cold chicken and cutlets, and all sorts of delicious sweets and fruit, and we all ate a lot, and groaned and said how ill we should be in the morning, and then ate some more and didn't care a bit. It was almost as good as a feast in the dormitory. Then we told funny stories, and asked riddles, and Lady Mary sang coon songs to her mandoline, and I was enjoying myself simply awfully when someone said—it was Mr Nash, and I shall never forgive him for it—

"Now it's your turn, Miss Una! Your father is always talking of your singing, yet we never seem to hear you. Too bad, you know! You can't refuse to-night, when we are all doing our best to amuse each other. Now, then, what is it to be?"

I was horrified! I love singing, but it seemed so formidable with no accompaniment, and no piano behind which to hide my blushes, but the more I protested, the more they implored, until Vere said quite sharply—

"For goodness' sake, child, do your best, and don't make a fuss! Nobody expects you to be a professional!"

"Start ahead, and I'll vamp an accompaniment. It will be better than nothing," said Lady Mary kindly, and Will whispered low in my ear: "Don't be nervous. Do your best. Astonish them, Babs!" And I did. That whisper inspired me somehow, and I sang "The Vale of Avoca," father's favourite ballad, pronouncing the words distinctly, as the singing mistress always made us do at school. I love the words, and the air is so sweet, and just suits my voice. I always feel quite worked up and choky when I come to the last verse, but I try not to show it, for it looks so silly to cry at yourself.

There was quite a burst of applause when I finished. The men clapped and called out "Bravo! Bravo!" Lady Mary said, "You little wretch! You do take the wind out of my sails. Fancy having to be bothered to sing with a voice like that! Gracious! I should never leave off!" and Vere laughed, and said in her sweetest tones, "But, for pity's sake, don't turn sentimental, Babs! It's so absurdly out of keeping! Stick to something lively and stirring—something from the comic operas! That would be far more in your line, don't you think so, Mr Dudley?"

Will was leaning back on his elbow, resting his head on his hand.

"It's a question of taste," he said lazily. "Some people are fond of comic operas. Personally, I detest them; but I don't profess to be a judge. I only know what I like."

"A sentimental ballad, for example?"

"Occasionally. Not always, by any means." He seemed determined not to give a straight-forward answer, and Vere turned aside with a shrug and began to talk to Mr Carstairs. She always takes refuge with him when other people fail her. I felt all hot and churned up with the excitement of singing, and then with rage at being snubbed in that public fashion. It spoiled all the pleasure and made me wonder if I had really made an exhibition of myself, and they were only pretending to be pleased.

The others were chattering like magpies; only Will Dudley and I were silent. I felt his eyes watching me, but I wouldn't look at him for quite a long time, till at last I simply had to turn round, when he smiled, such a kind nice smile, and said —

"Well, better now? Got the better of the little temper?"

"I don't know; partly, I suppose, but I do hate to be snubbed. I didn't want to sing. I did it to be polite; and it's horrid to think I made an idiot of myself."

Silence. It was no use. I *had* to ask him —

"Did I make an idiot of myself?"

"You know you didn't."

"Did you—did you think it was nice?"

"Yes."

That was all. Not another word could I get out of him, but I felt better, for it sounded as if he really meant it, and I cared for his opinion most of all.

Chapter Eight.

August 15th.

It is three weeks since the moonlight picnic, and so many things have happened since then, such awful, terrible things, that I don't know how to begin to tell them. I didn't think when I began this diary how thrilling it was going to be before I'd got half way through; but you never know what is going to happen in this world. It's awful how suddenly things come. I don't think I can ever again feel confident and easy-going, as I used to do. You read in books sometimes, "She was no longer a girl, she was a woman," and it is like that with me. Everything seems different and more solemn, and I don't think I can ever frivol again in quite the same whole-hearted way.

To begin at the beginning: we had a very lively time for the next week, and I grew quite fond of Vere's friends, even Lady Mary, whom I hated at first, and they all made a fuss of me, and made me sing every night till I felt quite proud. I invited Rachel over and over again, but she would never accept our invitations; but Will came often, either to dinner or lunch, or for an odd call, and Vere neglected everyone for him, and was so fascinating that I was in terror all the time. He admired her, of course; he would have been blind if he hadn't, but I could not decide if he liked her or not. Sometimes I saw him smiling to himself in the queer, half-scornful way he had done when they first met, and then I was sure he did not; but at other times he would watch her about the room, following every movement as if he couldn't help himself, and that's a bad sign. Lorna has a sister who is married, and she knew the man was going to propose, because he looked like that. Somehow I never had a chance of a quiet talk, when I could have given him a hint, and it was thinking about that and wondering how I could see him alone which made me suddenly remember that it was a whole week and more since I had been a walk with father. I went hot all over at the thought. It was ghastly to remember how I had planned and promised to be his companion, and to care for him first of all, and then to realise how I had forsaken him at the very first temptation!

He was so sweet about it, too, never complaining or seeming a bit vexed. Parents are really angels. It must be awful to have a child, and take such trouble with it all its life, and then to be neglected for strangers. I hadn't the heart to write in my diary that night. I was too ashamed. I was worse than Vere, for I had posed as being so good and dutiful. I won't make any more vows, but I confess here with that I am a selfish pig, and I am ashamed of myself.

The next morning I could hardly wait until breakfast was over, I was so anxious to be off. I got my cap and ran down to the stable and slipped my arm in father's as he stood talking to Vixen. He gave a little start of surprise—it hurt me, that start!—looked down at me and said, smiling—

"Well, dear, what is it?"

"Nothing. I'm coming with you!" I said, and he squeezed my hand against his side.

"Thank you, dear, but I'm going a long round. I won't be back until lunch. Better not leave your friends for so long."

"Vere is with them, father. I want to come."

"What's the matter? Not had a quarrel, have you? Has Vere been—"

"No, no, she hasn't! *Nothing* is the matter, except that I want you, and nobody else. Oh, father, don't be so horribly kind! Scold me—call me a selfish wretch! I know I have neglected you, dear. There was always something to do, and I—forgot, but really and truly I remembered all the time. It isn't nonsense, father, it's true. Can you understand?"

"I've been nineteen myself, Babs; I understand. Don't worry, darling. I missed you, but I was glad that you were happy, and I knew your heart was in the right place. We won't say anything more about it, but have a jolly walk and enjoy ourselves."

Oh, it is good to have someone who understands! If he had scolded or been reproachful I should have felt inclined to make excuses, but when he was so sweet and good I just loved him with all my heart, and prayed to be a better daughter to him all my life.

We had lovely walks after that, and on the third morning we met Will Dudley, and once again he and I sat on a log waiting for father while he interviewed a tenant. My heart quite thumped with agitation as I thought that now was the time to lead the conversation skilfully round to Vere, and insinuate delicately that she had a mania for making people fall in love with her, and that it didn't always mean as much as it seemed when she was sweet and gushing. It wasn't exactly an easy thing to do, but you can't be a guardian angel without a little trouble.

"So you have torn yourself away from your friends this morning," he said at last. "How is it that you were allowed to escape? What is the special campaign for killing time to-day, if one may ask?"

"You may ask, but it's rude to be sarcastic. You are often lazy yourself, though in a different fashion. You love to lie on your back on the grass and do nothing but browse and stare up at the sky. You have told me so many times."

"Ah, but what of my thoughts? Under a semblance of ease I am in reality working out the most abstruse problems. I did not mean to be sarcastic; I inquired in all seriousness how your valuable company could be spared."

"For the best of all reasons—because nobody wanted it! Captain Grantly wants Lady Mary, Lady Mary wants Captain Grantly. Miss Talbot wants someone she can't get, but it doesn't happen to be me; the rest all want Vere, and have no thought for anyone else. Men always do want to be with Vere. Wherever she goes they fall in love with her and follow her about. She is so lovely, and she—she likes to be liked. Everyone says she is so charming and irresistible—they have told her so since she was a child—and she likes to prove that it was true. If—if anyone seems to like anyone else better it—sort of—worries her, and makes her feel neglected."

"I see."

"Then, of course, she is extra specially nice, and seems to be more interested in him than anyone else."

"Pleasant for him!"

"It is, for a time. But if he trusted to it and believed that she was really in earnest, he might get to care himself, and then, when he found out, he would be disappointed."

"Naturally so."

"It has happened like that before, several times, and sometimes there are other people to be considered—I mean there might be another girl whom the man had liked before, and when he had given her up, and found that-that—"

"That he had given up the substance and grasped the shadow—"

"Yes; then, of course, they would both be miserable, and it would be worse than ever."

"Naturally it would be."

He spoke in the same cool, half-jeering tone, then suddenly turned round and bent his head down to mine, staring at me with bright grey eyes.

"Why not be honest, Babs, and not beat about the bush? You think that my peace is threatened and want to warn me of it, isn't that it, now? You are my very good friend, and I am grateful for your interest. Did you think I was in danger?"

"Sometimes—once or twice! Don't be angry. I know you would be true and loyal, but sometimes—I saw you watching her—"

"She is very lovely, Babs; the loveliest woman I have ever seen. There was some excuse for that."

"I know, I feel it myself, and it was just because I could understand a little that I spoke. I thought quite likely that you might be angry at first, but it was better that you should be that than wretched in the end."

"Quite so; but I am not angry at all, only very grateful for your bravery in tackling a difficult subject. I have a pretty good opinion of myself, but I am only a man, and other men have imagined themselves secure and found out their mistake before now. Forewarned is forearmed. Thank you for the warning," and he smiled at me with a sudden flash of the eyes which left me hot and breathless.

Was I in time? Had he really begun to care for Vere so soon as this? I longed to say more, but dared not. All my courage had gone, and I was thankful when father came out of the cottage and put an end to our *tête-à-tête*.

I thought there would be a difference after this, but there wasn't—not a bit. When Will came to the house he was as nice as ever to Vere, and seemed quite willing to be monopolised as much as she liked. If he avoided anyone it was me, and I was not a bit surprised. People may say what they like, but they do bear you a grudge for giving them good advice. I sat in a corner and made cynical reflections to myself, and nobody took any notice of me, and I felt more cynical than ever, and went to my bedroom and banged about the furniture to relieve my feelings.

Vere came into my room soon after, and stood by the window talking while I brushed my hair. The blind was up, for it was moonlight and I hate to shut it out. Her dress was of some soft silvery stuff, and, standing there in the pale blue light, she looked oh, so lovely, more like a fairy than a human creature! I am so glad I admired her then; I'm glad I told her that I did; I'm glad, glad, glad that I was nice and loving as a sister ought to be, and that we kissed and put our arms round each other when we said good night.

"Sleep well, little girl, you look tired. We can't let you lose your bonny colour," she said, in her, pretty caressing way; nobody can be as sweet as Vere when she likes.

I was tired, but I sat by the window for quite a long time after she left, thinking, thinking, thinking. I can't tell what I thought exactly, so many things passed through my head, and when I said my prayers I hardly said any words at all; I just put down my head and trusted God to understand me better than I did myself. I had so much to make me happy, but I was not happy somehow. I had so much to make me content, yet there was something missing that made everything else seem blank. I wanted to be good, and such horrid, envious feelings rose up in my heart. In my dear little room, at my own dear little table, I asked God to help me, and to take care of me whatever happened.

And He did, but it was not in the way I expected.

At last the moon disappeared behind the clouds which had been gathering for some time, and I went to bed and fell fast asleep as soon as my head touched the pillow, as I always do, no matter how agitated I am. I suppose it's being nineteen and in such good health. "How long I slept I cannot tell," as they say in ghost stories, but suddenly I woke up with a start and a sort of horrid feeling that something was wrong. The room felt close and heavy, and there was a curious noise coming from outside the door, a sort of buzzing, crackling noise. I didn't get up at once, for I felt stupid and heavy; it was a minute or two before I seemed really able to think, and then— oh, I shall never forget that moment!—I knew what it was. I felt it! I went cold all over, and my legs shook under me as I stepped on to the floor.

The air was thick, and it smelt. My door was the nearest to the staircase, and when I opened it a great cloud of smoke rolled in my face. For a moment it was all cloud and darkness, then a light shot up from below, and the crackling noise was repeated. It was true, quite true. The house was on fire, and already the staircase was ablaze!

Chapter Nine.

August 16th.

We used to wonder at school sometimes how we should behave if we suddenly found ourselves in a position of great danger. I always said I should scream and hide my face, and faint if I possibly could, but I am thankful to remember that, when it came to the point, I did nothing of the sort. My heart gave one big, sickening throb, and then I felt suddenly quite calm and cold and self-possessed, almost as if I didn't care. I went back into my room, put on my dressing-gown and slippers, took up a big brass bell which one of the girls had given me, and, shutting the door carefully behind me, ran along the corridor, ringing it as loudly as I could, and knocking at each door as I passed. I didn't call out "Fire!"—it was too terrifying; besides, I knew the others would guess what was wrong as soon as they heard the bell and smelt the smoke, and, in less than two minutes, every door was open, and the occupants of the different rooms first peeped and then rushed out on to the landing in dressing-gowns and shawls, and all sorts of quaint-looking wraps. One light was always left burning all night long, so we could see each other, even when the smoke hid that other horrible lurid light, and it is wonderful how brave we all were on the whole. Mother came forward wrapped in her long blue gown, and found a chair for Madge Talbot, who was the only one who showed signs of breaking down, just as quietly and graciously as if she had been entertaining her in the drawing-room. Father and the men consulted rapidly together, and Vere put her arm round me, and leant on my shoulder. I could feel her trembling, but she shut her lips tight, and tried hard to smile encouragingly at poor Madge, and all the time the smoke grew thicker, and the horrid crackling louder and nearer.

"The drawing-room!" we heard father say. "The servants have been careless in putting out the lights, and something has smouldered and finally caught the curtains—that's the most probable explanation. If that is the case, I fear the back stairs will be impassable; they are even nearer than these."

He turned and ran quickly down the passage, followed by Captain Grantly and Mr Nash. Mr Carstairs came and stood by Vere's side, as if he could not bear to leave her unprotected, and she looked up at him and smiled a white little smile, as if she were glad to have him there. A moment later the men came back, and, as father turned and closed the heavy oak door which divided one wing from another, we knew without asking that the other staircase was also cut off.

Madge began to sob hysterically, but father stopped her with a wave of his hand, and said sharply, addressing us all—

"The back staircase is impracticable, but if we keep our senses, there is no real danger to fear. I have rung the alarm bell, and the men will soon be round with ropes and ladders. The best thing you can do is to go back to your rooms, dress rapidly, and collect a few valuables which can be lowered from the window. You can have five minutes—no longer. I will ring a bell at the end of that time, and we will all meet in my room, which is the centre position, and therefore the farthest from the fire. Now, girls, quick! There is no time to lose!"

We ran. Some time—in a long, long time to come—we shall laugh to think what curious costumes we made! It was just the first thing that came to hand. I was decently clothed in two minutes, seized a dressing-bag, put in my pearl necklace, a few odd trinkets, this diary, and the old Bible I have had since I was ten years old, and rushed along to mother's room to see if I could help.

She was putting on a long dark coat, and had a lace scarf tied over her hair. Even then, in the middle of the night, she looked dignified and beautiful, and her eyes melted in the tender way they have at great moments as she saw me.

"Ready, daughter?" she said smiling, and then came up and took me into her arms. "Good girl! Brave girl! We must help the others, Una. You and I have no time to be afraid."

"Thank you, mother darling!" I said, gratefully, for I had been, oh, terribly afraid, and it was just the best thing she could have said to calm me and give me courage; and, while we clung together, father came hurrying in. He hardly seemed to notice me, Babs, his pet daughter!—He looked only at mother, and spoke to her.

"Are you warm, Carina? Are you suitably dressed? You must have no train—nothing to make movement difficult. That's all right. Don't trust yourself to anyone but me, sweet-heart! I'll come to you in good time!"

"Yes, Boy, yes! I'll come with you," said mother softly.

They went out of the room arm-in-arm, never once looking at me. It seemed as if at the first touch of danger they had gone back to the old days when they were lovers, and no difference of interest had arisen to draw them apart. It made the tears come to my eyes to see them, and I was glad to be forgotten.

The women servants were all awake by now, and, finding their own staircase in flames, came swarming down the corridor to escape by the main way; when they found this also was impracticable, they began to shriek and moan, and to implore us to save them, and it was hard work to get them into one room and keep them quiet. The men crowded at the window, looking for help, and shouting directions to the coachmen and gardeners when at last they came running towards the house. They flew off, some to get ropes and ladders, some to alarm the neighbourhood, and bring help from the nearest fire office. It was three miles off, and in the country firemen are scattered about in outlying cottages, and there would be all the way to come back. It made one sick to think how long it might be before the engine arrived; and meantime the fire was steadily spreading on the ground floor. When father bent forward to shout to the men, the light on his face was dreadful to see. I had a horrible longing to scream, and I think I should have done it if I hadn't been so occupied with Annie, the kitchen-maid, who was literally almost mad with fright. It seemed to soothe her to hold my arm, poor little soul. Respect for "the gentry" had been so instilled into her from her earliest years that I honestly believe she imagined the very flames would hesitate to touch the Squire's "darter!"

It seemed ages before William and James came back—without the ladders! They were kept locked up by father's special orders, as so many jewel burglaries had taken place in the neighbourhood, the thieves using ladders to get into a bedroom while dinner was going on downstairs. Now, in the usual contrary way of things, the man who had the key had ridden away, forgetting all about it in his haste to bring help. Father stamped with impatience while the men were reporting their failure and asking further instructions. It was getting more and more difficult to hear, with that horrid roar coming up from below, and Mr Carstairs said suddenly—

"We can't waste time like this! These men have lost their heads. Grantly, you and I are strongest. We must get down and break in the door. Come to the back of the house; there must surely be some way of dropping down on an out-house."

"The blue room—over the larder. It's a deep drop, but safe enough for fellows like you. I'll show you!" cried father promptly, and led the way forward. It was no time to protest or to make polite speeches. Something had to be done, and done at once. I watched them go and envied them. It's hardest of all to be a woman and have to wait. I would rather a hundred times have faced that drop than have sat in that room listening to the noise, seeing Vere growing whiter and whiter, and mother's face grow old and lined. If the worst came to the worst, I would go and sit beside them, but for the present I held Annie's hand and stroked it, and wondered if it could be true that life was really going to end like this. Only nineteen, and just home from school—it seemed so young to die! I remembered Will, and wondered if he would be sorry, and if he and Rachel would talk of me when they were married. Then I forgot everything, and lust shut my eyes and prayed, prayed, prayed.

A great shout of relief and joy! Father and Mr Nash were leaning out of the window waving their hands to the other men, who were carrying the ladders across the lawn. We all sobbed with relief, for it seemed as if escape must be easy now, but the ladders were not long enough, they had to be tied together, and by this time the flames were leaping out of the window below; we could see the light dancing up and down, and it seemed a dreadful prospect to have to pass them on an open ladder. I looked at mother—mother who never walked a step outside the grounds, who was waited upon hand and foot, and spent half her time lying on the sofa. It seemed impossible that she could attempt such a feat!

The moment the ladder was fixed father turned round and called to us to come forward, but we all hung back silent and trembling. Then he stamped his foot, and his eyes flashed.

"Are you going to turn cowards and risk other lives besides your own? There is not a moment to lose. Every moment will make it more formidable. Mary, you are a brave girl! Will you lead the way?"

She walked forward without a word. I did admire her! Father lifted her up; a pair of arms were thrust out to receive her from the midst of the clouds of smoke. We all held our breath for what seemed an age, but was only a few minutes, I suppose, and then came another cheer, and we knew she was safe. The servants rushed forward at that, but when they looked down and saw the flames licking the very side of the ladder, they shrieked again and fell back; so Madge went next, and then father walked up to mother and took her by the hand. She looked up at him and shook her head.

"Not yet, dear, not yet. The girls first!" she said, but he wouldn't listen to that.

"The girls wouldn't go before you. You can't stand this any longer. I am going to carry you down and come back for them. Come, sweetheart!"

She rose then without a word, and we saw him lift her in one arm like a baby and let himself down slowly, slowly with the other hand.

Oh, the awfulness of that moment when they both disappeared and we were left alone! With father gone it seemed as if there were no one left to keep order or inspire us with any show of courage. I think we all went mad or something like it, and, before we knew what was happening, one of the servants had opened the door and flown shrieking along the passage. Another great gust of smoke rushed into the room; we could hardly see each other; we were all rushing about, jostling together, fighting like wild things for air and freedom.

"Vere, Vere!" I shouted, and she clutched at my arm, and we ran together down the corridor, to the head of the servants' stairs, back again faster than ever into the blue room where the men had let themselves down to the roof of the larder. There seemed just a chance that we might be able to do the same. It was the only chance I could think of, and Vere was clinging to me, begging me to save her, and not let her be burnt.

"I can't die, Babs—I can't! I've never thought of it. I'm frightened! Oh, Babs, Babs, think of something—think of a way—Save me! Save me!"

"I'll try, Vere, but you must help, you must be quiet! The heat is not so bad here, and if we get on the roof and call, someone may hear us. They will come to look if they find we have gone. Oh, we should never have left that room! Father trusted us to wait for him, but it is too late now... Look, here's a sheet: we must tear it into strips and make a rope. It will be easier that way."

But when they tell you in books to make ropes of sheets, they forget that it's almost impossible to tear strong new sheets, and that one cannot always find scissors in a strange room in the middle of the night. In the end, we could only knot the two together, and tie one end to the rail of the washstand. It was not long enough then, but I scrambled out and let myself down to the end, and then dropped, and by good providence managed to steady myself on the roof beneath. It was not so very sloping as roofs go, and the gutter was deep, and made a kind of little wall round the edge. I called to Vere to follow, and promised to catch her, but it took, oh, ages of coaxing and scolding before she would venture, and it was only by a miracle that we didn't both fall to the ground, for she let go so suddenly and clutched at me in such frantic terror when I stretched up to catch her.

We didn't fall, however, but cowered down together on the roof with our feet fixed firmly against the projecting gutter, and I, for one, felt in a worse position than ever. We were still too far from the ground to jump down without hurting ourselves on the hard paving stones, and no one was in sight, no one heard our calls for help. To make things worse, in getting nearer the ground we had come nearer to the fire itself, for some of the windows on the ground floor had fallen in, and it was just like looking into the heart of a furnace. There is nothing more awful than the speed with which fire travels. One feels so utterly helpless before it. The tiles on which we sat were hot. I don't know if it was fancy, but every now and then I seemed to feel a movement beneath us as if something might give way. I think now that it really was nervousness, for the roof was left practically unhurt, but at the time anything seemed possible, and I was terrified. We called and called again, but no one came, and it seemed as if hours passed by, and the fire came creeping nearer and nearer. Sometimes Vere would be frantic with excitement; sometimes she would cover her face with her hands and moan; sometimes she would be on the brink of fainting. I began to see that if something was not done at once she would faint, and then we would probably both fall to the ground together and be killed outright. Something had to be done, and I had to do it. I went creepy cold all down my spine, for I knew what it was I had to do, and was in mortal terror of facing it.

Somehow or other, if Vere were to be saved in time, I must get up from my cramped seat, lower myself over the edge of the roof, hang at full length from the coping and drop on to the flags beneath. The men had done it, but they were men, and it was a big drop even for them, and they haven't got nerves like girls, or skirts, or slippers with heels. I was frightened out of my wits, but I knew that every moment I thought about it I should be more frightened still, so I just told Vere what I was going to do—and did it!

I can't write about it; it makes me feel queer even now! The awful moment when you get over and swing into space; and the feeling that you must look down, the ache in your hands as you cling on, and the terror of leaving go! Mental pain is worse than physical, so it was really a relief to reach the ground, even though one foot did go over, and a pain like a red-hot poker shot up the leg. I thought I had broken the foot to pieces, but it was only the ankle that was sprained, and I could limp along, in a fashion, though so slowly that it took ages to get round to the front of the house. At another time I suppose I should have sat still and howled; but you don't think of pain when it is a case of life and death, and I knew there was no time to spare.

It could not really have been very long since we left father's room, but already the scene was quite changed. The alarm bell had roused the neighbourhood, and there was quite a little crowd on the lawn. I saw at a glance how it was that we had not been missed. The servants had rushed upstairs to the third storey, and were grouped together at a window there screaming and calling for help, while the poor men worked hard at lengthening the ladders. At a distance, and through the clouds of smoke, it was impossible to distinguish one figure from another, and everyone had taken for granted that we were there with the rest. Nobody noticed me hobbling forward till I got close up to the workers, and saw a well-known grey figure busy with the ropes. I pulled at his arm, and he lifted a white face, then leapt to his feet and seized me by both hands.

"You, Una! Here! Thank God! How is it possible? Which way did you come?"

"Out of a window—but, oh, don't talk—you must save Vere first! Round at the back—now—at once! I'll show you the way, but I can't walk, my foot is hurt—"

I felt as if I could not keep up a moment longer, but Will picked me up in his arms as if I had been a baby, and said soothingly—

"There! Now think quietly for one moment, and tell me what we shall want! Where is she - high up? Shall I get some of these men to help."

"She's on an outhouse roof. I dropped down, but it hurt me, you see, and Vere daren't attempt it. A ladder would do, just one ladder. There's Mr Carstairs—he'll come! I'll tell him where to go."

I did tell him, and the poor fellow's face of mingled rapture and fear was touching to see; then Will went on in front, still carrying me in his arms, while the others followed with ladders and sheets and all kinds of things that might be needed. I was moaning to myself all the time, and Will put down his head and said tenderly—

"Does it hurt so much, poor little girl?"

But it was my heart which hurt; I was so terrified of what we were going to find.

She was still there. I lifted my head as we came round the corner of the house, and I could see her. She was not sitting as when I had left, but half standing, half crouching forward, her hands stretched out, her hair loose over her shoulders. She looked like a mad woman; she *was* mad, poor Vere, and the sight of us in the distance seemed to excite her more than ever. We called to her; we begged her to be calm, to sit still for one moment—just one moment longer. The men ran forward to reassure her, but she didn't understand—she seemed past understanding. Just as help was within reach she threw out her arms with a dreadful cry and jumped, and her foot caught in the coping as she fell. Oh, I can't write about it! I must forget, or I shall go mad myself!...

Chapter Ten.

August 16th.

They picked her up, poor Vere! the man who loved her, and the servants who had known her since she was a child; picked her up and laid her on a board which did duty for a stretcher, rolled up a pillow for her head, and drew her golden hair back from her face. Mr Carstairs took off his coat and laid it over her as she lay. His face was as white as hers, and all drawn with pain, while hers was quite still and quiet. So still! I was afraid to look at her, or to ask any questions.

Will put me down in a corner, and I sat there trembling and sick at heart, watching the little procession go round the corner of the house. I thought they had forgotten me, and I didn't care. I was past caring! The pain and the shock and excitement were making me quite faint and rambly in the head, when someone spoke to me suddenly, and put an arm round my neck.

"It's all over, darling! We have come to take you home. All your troubles are over now," said a soft voice, and I looked up and saw a face looking down at me inside a close-fitting hood. For a moment I did not recognise her; I thought it was a nun or someone like that sprung out of a hazy dream, but when she smiled I knew it was Rachel, and somehow I began to cry at once, not because I was sorry, but because now that she was there I could afford to give way. She would look after Vere.

"Yes, cry, dear, it will do you good; but you mustn't stay here any longer. We have brought a chair, and are going to put you in it, and carry you home to the Grange. We are your nearest neighbours, so you must give us the pleasure of looking after you for a time. They are taking your sister on ahead, and a man has ridden off for a doctor. He will look after that poor foot of yours presently. I am afraid it will be painful for you to be moved, but we will be very careful. The servants are preparing rooms in case they are needed. You shall get straight to bed."

"And mother and father?"

"Your mother was taken to the Lodge. She is well, but very exhausted. They want to keep her quiet to-night. Your father knows you are safe. He is very thankful, but he will not leave his post until the servants are safe. Now here is the chair, and here are Will and the coach-man waiting to carry you. Are you ready to be moved?"

I set my teeth and said "Yes," and they hoisted me up and carried me down the path after that other dreadful procession. Oh, my foot! I never knew what pain was like before that. How do people go on bearing it day after day, week after week, year after year? I couldn't! I should go mad. I would have shrieked then, but my pride wouldn't let me before Will and Rachel, when they kept praising me, and saying how brave I was.

I was carried straight to a room and put to bed. Rachel bathed and bandaged my ankle, and then hurried away, and no one came near me for an age. I knew why. They were all with Vere; my ankle was a trifle compared with her injuries. When at last the doctor did appear, he could tell me very little about her. The great thing was to keep her quiet until the next day, when he would be able to make an examination. I summoned courage to ask if she were in danger, and he answered me rather strangely—

"In danger—of death, do you mean? Certainly not, so far as I can tell."

What other danger could there be? I lay and pondered over it all through that hot, aching night; but I have learnt since then that there are many things which may seem, oh, far, far harder than death to a young, beautiful girl. I have never had a great dread of death, I am thankful to say. Why should one fear it? If you really and truly are a Christian, and believe what you pretend, it's unreasonable to dread going to a life which is a thousand times better and happier; and as for dying itself, I've talked to hospital nurses when I was ill at school, and they say that most people know nothing about it, but are only very, very tired, and fall asleep. Of course, there are exceptions. It would have been dreadful to have been burnt alive!

I did sleep towards morning, and it was so odd waking up in that strange room, which I had hardly noticed in the pain and confusion of the night before. I smiled a little even then as I looked round. It was so Racheley! Lots of nice things badly arranged, so different from my dear little room! Oh, my dear little room; should I ever, ever see it again? Someone was sitting behind the curtains, and as I moved he bent forward and took hold of my hand. It was father, looking so white and old that the tears came to my eyes to see him; but he was alive and safe, that was the great thing, and able to tell me that all the servants had been saved, and to give a good report of mother.

"Very weak and shaken, but nothing more than that, thank God! Good old Mrs Rogers is very happy helping Terese to nurse her. She sent you her love."

"And, oh, father, the house, the dear old home? Is it quite ruined, or did you manage to put out the fire before it went too far? What happened after we left?"

His face set, but he said calmly—

"The lower rooms are more or less destroyed, but the second storey is little injured, except by smoke and, of course, water. The engines worked well, and we had more help than we could use. The people turned out nobly. The home itself can be saved, Babs; it will take months to repair, but it can be done, and we shall be thankful to keep the old roof above our heads."

"But it will never look the same. The ivy that has been growing for hundreds of years will be dead, and all the beautiful creepers! I can't imagine 'The Moat' with bare walls. And inside—oh, poor father, all your treasures gone! The silver and the china, and the cases of curios, and the old family portraits! You were so proud of them. Doesn't it break your heart to lose them all?"

"No," he said quietly, "I cannot think of such things to-day. I am too filled with thankfulness that out of all that big household not a life has been lost, and that my three darlings are with me still. Those things you speak of are precious in their way, but I have no room for regret for them in my heart when a still greater treasure is in danger, Vere—"

"Oh, father, tell me about Vere! Tell me the truth. I am not a child, and I ought to know. How has she hurt herself?"

"Truthfully, dear, no one knows. She cannot move, and there is evidently some serious injury, but what it is cannot be decided until after an examination. They fear some spinal trouble."

Spinal! I had a horrid vision of plaster jackets and invalid couches, and those long flat, dreadful-looking chairs which you meet being wheeled about at Bournemouth. It seemed impossible to connect such things with Vere!

"It can't be so bad! It can't be really serious," I cried vehemently. "It was all over in such a second, and we were there at once; everything was done for her! Vere is easily upset, and she feels stiff and strained. I do myself, but she will be better soon, father—they must make her better! She could not bear to be ill."

He sighed so heavily, poor father, and leant his head against the wall as if he were worn out, body and mind.

"Poor Vere, poor darling! I often wondered how her discipline would come. Pray God it may not be this way; but if it does come thus we must help her through it as bravely as may be. It will be hard for us as well as for her; terribly hard for your mother especially. We shall look to you, Babs, to cheer us up; you are young and lighthearted, and if our fears come true you will have a great work before you."

But I didn't feel that I could promise at all. After he had gone I lay thinking it all over and feeling perfectly wretched at the idea of being cheerful under such circumstances. I can be as lively as a grig, (what is a grig, by the way?) when things go smoothly, and other people are cheerful, too, but to keep lively when they are in the depths of woe, and you have to keep things going all by yourself and there is no excitement or variety, is a very different thing. I am quelled at once by sighs, and tears, and solemn faces. It's my nature, I can't help it. I'm so sensitive. Miss Bruce once said that that word "sensitive" was often used when "selfish" would be much more applicable. I thought it horrid of her at the time, but I expect, like most hard things, it is true. Now if you didn't think of yourself at all but only and wholly of others, it would be your one aim through life to make them happy, and no effort would be too difficult if it succeeded in doing that. Then people would talk about you and say you were "the sunshine of the home," and your parents would bless you with their latest breath, and people who had misjudged you would flock round and sit at your knee, and profit by your example. I should like to be like that. It would be so lovely and so soothing to the feelings.

The doctor came at noon and allowed me to be lifted on to the sofa and wheeled into the next room. It made a change, but it was a very long day, all the same, and I thought the afternoon would never come to an end. Rachel came in and out the room, but could never settle down, for as soon as she sat down, rat-tat came to the door, someone said, "Miss Rachel, please," and off she flew to do something else.

Mrs Greaves brought some sewing and sat beside me, but she can't talk, poor dear; she can only make remarks at intervals and sigh between them, and it isn't cheerful. At tea-time Mr Greaves appeared, and—well, he *is* a curious creature! I have always been taught that it is mean to accept hospitality, "eat salt," as the proverb has it, and then speak unkindly of your host, and, of course, I wouldn't to anyone else, but to you, O diary, I must confess that I'm truly and devoutly thankful he is not my father.

He has a great big face, and a great big voice, and very little manners, and I believe he enjoys, really thoroughly enjoys, bullying other people, and seeing them miserable. He was quite nice to me in the way of sympathising with my foot, and saying that he was pleased to see me; but I felt inclined to shake him when he went on to speak of "The Moat," and of all we had done that we should not have done, and left undone that we should have done, and of what *he* would have done in our place; making out, if you please, that the fire was all our fault, and that we deserved it if we *were* burnt out of house and home!

Rachel poured tea on the troubled waters, and he snubbed her for her pains and called his wife "madam," and wished to know if she had nothing fit to eat to offer to her guest. There were about ten different things on the table already; it was only rage which kept me from eating, but he chose to pretend that everything was bad, and we had a lively time of it, while he ate some of the cakes on every plate in turns and took a second helping and finished it to the last crumb, and then declared that it wasn't fit for human consumption. All the while poor Mrs Greaves sat like a mute at a funeral, hanging her head and never saying so much as "Bo!" in self-defence; and Rachel smiled as if she were listening to a string of compliments, and said—

"Try the toast, then, father dear. It is nice and crisp, just as you like it. If you don't like those cakes, we won't have them again. Ready for some more tea, dear? It is stronger now that it has stood a little while."

"It might easily be that. Hot water bewitched—that's what I call your tea, young lady. Waste of good cream and sugar—"

So it went on—grumble, grumble, grumble, grum— And that Rachel actually put her arm round his neck and kissed his cross red face.

"It is not the tea that is bad, dear, it is your poor old foot. Cheer up! It will be better to-morrow. This new medicine is said to work wonders."

Then he exploded for another half hour about doctors and medicines, abusing them both as hard as he could, and at the end pointed to my face, which, to judge from my feelings, must have been chalky green, and wanted to know if they called themselves nurses, and if they wished to kill me outright, for if they did they had better say so at once, and let him know what was in store. He had borne enough in the last twenty-five years, goodness knew!

I was carried back to bed and cried surreptitiously beneath the clothes while Rachel tidied up.

"Dear father," she said fondly; "he is a martyr to gout. It is so sad for him to have an illness which depresses his spirits and spoils his enjoyment. There are so few pleasures left to him in life now, but he bears it wonderfully well."

I peeped at her over the sheet, but her face was quite grave and serious. She meant it, every word!

Chapter Eleven.

August 17th.

I was wheeled into the library every day, and lay in state upon the sofa, receiving callers. Mother drove over each afternoon for a short visit. Will came in often, and brought Mr Carstairs with him. The other members of Vere's house-party had returned home, but this poor, good fellow could not tear himself away from the neighbourhood until the doctor had come to some more definite conclusion about Vere.

A specialist had been down from town, and he pronounced the spine injured by the fall, but hoped that, with complete rest, recovery was possible in the future. How long would she have to rest? It was impossible to say. If he said a year, it would probably be exciting false hopes; it might be two years, or even three. And at the end of that time, even of the longest time, was there any certainty? It was impossible to be certain in such cases, but the probabilities made for improvement. Miss Sackville had youth on her side, and a good constitution. It was a mistake to look on the dark side. "Hope, my dear sir, hope is a more powerful medicine than people realise! Fifty guineas, please—thank you! Train leaves at two o'clock, I think you said?"

I was thankful I had not to tell Vere the verdict. Father broke it to her, and said she "took it calmly," but he looked miserable, and every time he went to see her he looked still more wretched and *baffled*. There is no other word to express it. He seems impatient for me to see her, and when at last I could hobble to the door of her room, went with me and whispered urgently, "Try what you can make of her! Don't avoid the subject. It is better sometimes to speak out," and I went in, feeling almost as anxious as he was himself.

Vere was lying in bed, with her hair twisted loosely on the top of her head, and wearing one of her pretty blue jackets, all ribbons and frilly-willies. In a way she looked just the same; in a way so different that I might never have seen her before. The features were the same, but the expression was new; it was not that she looked troubled, or miserable, or cross, or anything like that; you could not tell what she felt; it was just as if a mask covered everything that you wanted to see, and left only the mere bare outline.

She spoke first.

"Well, Una! So your foot is better, and you can get about? I was so sorry to hear it was bad. I suppose you are not able to get out yet?"

"Oh, no! This is my longest walk. I am afraid of attempting the stairs. The Greaves are very kind. I believe they like having us here."

"Having you, you mean. I am sure you must make a delightful break in the monotony. As for me,"—she thrust out her hands with an expressive little grimace—"I have been rather a nuisance to everybody while these stupid doctors have been debating over the case. It's a comfort that they have made up their minds at last, and that I can be moved as soon as there is a place ready for me. Father is ordering a spinal carriage from London with the latest conveniences, like the suburban villas. I believe you lie on a mattress or something of the sort, which can be lifted and put down in the carriage. Such a saving of trouble! It is wonderful how cleverly they manage things nowadays."

Just the old, light, airy voice; just the same society drawl. She might have been talking of a new ball dress for any sign of emotion to be seen, and yet I know well that Vere—the old Vere—could have faced no fate more bitter than this! I stared at her, and she stared back with a fixed, unchanging smile. I knew by that smile that it was not resignation she felt; not anything like that lovely willing way in which really good people accept trouble—crippled old women in cottages, who will tell you how good God has been to them, when they are as poor as mice, and have never been out of one room for years; and other people who lose everybody they love best, and spend their lives trying to make other people happy, instead of glumping alone. I have really and truly known people like that, but their faces looked sweet and radiant. Vere's was very different. I knew now what father had been worrying about the last few days, and what he meant by advising me to speak openly, but it was not easy to do so. I was afraid of her with that new look!

"We are both cripples for the time being, but if I get strong before you do, I'll do everything I can to help you, dear, and make the time pass quickly," I was beginning feebly, when she caught me up at once, as if she did not want to hear any more.

"Oh, thanks; but I love lazing. I am quite an adept in the art of doing nothing, and you will have quite enough on your hands. It's a capital thing for you, my being out of the running. You would never have taken your proper place unless you were really forced into it. Now you will have to be Miss Sackville, and you must keep up my reputation and do credit to your training."

"I shall never take your place, Vere," I said sadly, and then something—I don't know what—reminded me suddenly of Mr Carstairs, and I asked if she knew he was staying with Will.

"Oh, yes. He writes to me frequently—sheets upon sheets. He has made up his mind to stay until he can see me again, and realise that I am still in the flesh, so he will have the pleasure of seeing me in my new chair. I must send him an invitation to join me on my first expedition. He really deserves some reward for his devotion."

I had a vision of them as they would look. Vere stretched at full length, flat on her back, on that horrid-looking chair, and Mr Carstairs towering above her, with his face a-quiver with grief and pity, as I had seen it several times during the last week. If it had been me, I should have hated appearing before a lover in such a guise, and I am only an ordinary-looking girl, whereas Vere is a beauty, and has been accustomed to think of her own appearance before anything in the world. I could not understand her.

"I like Jim Carstairs," I said sturdily. "I hope some day I may have someone to care for me as he does for you, Vere. It must be a lovely feeling. He has been in such distress about you, and on that night—that awful night—I shall never forget his face—"

"Ah, you have an inconvenient memory, Babs! It was always your failing. For my part I mean to forget all about it as soon as possible. You were very good and brave, by the way, and, I am afraid, hurt your foot in trying to save me. I would rather not return to the subject, so I will just thank you once and for all, and express my gratitude. You practically saved my life. Think of it! If it had not been for you I should not have had a chance of lying here now, or riding about in my fine new chair!"

"Vere, *don't*! don't sneer!" I cried hotly, for the mask had slipped for a moment, and I had caught a glimpse of the bitter rebellion hidden beneath the smile. "It is awful for you—we are all wretched about it; but there is hope still, and the doctor says you will get better if only you will give yourself a chance. Why do you pretend? why smile and make fun when all the time—oh, I know it, I know it quite well—your heart is breaking!"

Her lip trembled. I thought she was going to break down, but in a moment she was composed again, saying in the same light, jeering tones—

"Would you prefer me to weep and wail? You have known me all your life; can you imagine me—Vere Sackville—lying about with red eyes and a swollen face, posing as an object of pity? Can you imagine me allowing myself to be pitied?"

"Not pitied, perhaps—no one likes that; but if people love you, and sympathise—"

"Bah!" She flicked her eyelids impatiently. I realised at that moment that she could not move her head, and it gave me a keener realisation of her state than I had had before. "Bah! It is all the same. I want nothing from my friends now that they did not give me a month ago. If I have to be on my back instead of walking about, it is no affair of theirs. I neither ask nor desire their commiseration. The kindest thing they can do is to leave me alone."

I thought of the old days when she was well and strong, and could run about as she liked, and how bored she was after a few days of quiet home life. How could she bear the long weeks and months stretched out motionless on a couch, with none of her merry friends to cheer her and distract her thoughts. The old Vere could not have borne it, but this was a new Vere whom I had never seen before. I felt in the dark concerning her and her actions.

We talked it over at tea that afternoon, Rachel and Will and I. He came to call, so Mr Greaves sent up a polite message that he preferred to remain in his own room, and, of course, his poor wife had to stay, too, so for once we young people were alone. I was a little embarrassed at being number three with a pair of lovers, as any nice-minded person would be. I did all I could for them—I pretended to be tired, and said I thought I'd better be wheeled back to my room, and I made faces at Rachel behind Will's back to show what I meant, but she only smiled, and he said—

"I can see you, Babs, and it's not becoming! We have no secrets to talk about, and would much rather have you with us, wouldn't we, Rachel?"

"Of course you are to stay, Una dear; don't say another word about it," Rachel answered kindly, but that wasn't exactly answering his question. She was too honest to say that she would rather have me there, and I don't think she quite liked his saying so, either, for she was even quieter than usual for the next five minutes. Then Will began to talk about Vere, and of Mr Carstairs' anxiety, and father's distress about her state of mind. He seemed to think that she did not realise what was before her, but Rachel and I knew better than that, and assured him that he need fear no rude awakening.

"Vere is not one of the people who deceive themselves for good or bad. She is very shrewd and far-seeing, and, though she may not say anything about it, I know she has thought of every single little difficulty and trouble that will have to be faced. When it comes to the point, you will see that she has her own ideas and suggestions, which will be better than any others. She will order us about, and tell us what clothes to choose, how to lift her, and where to take her. And she will do it just as she is doing things now, as calmly and coolly as if she had been accustomed to it all her life."

"Extraordinary!" cried Will. He put down his cup and paced up and down the floor, frowning till his eyebrows met. "Marvellous composure! I should not have believed it possible. A lovely girl like that to have her life wrecked in a moment; to look forward to being a hopeless invalid for years—perhaps for ever. It is enough to unhinge the strongest brain, and she bears it without a murmur, you say; realises it all and still keeps calm? You women are wonderful creatures. You teach us many lessons in submission."

Rachel and I looked at each other and were silent, but I knew that she knew, and I had a longing to hear what Will would say. Somehow, ever since knowing him I have always felt more satisfied when I knew his opinion on any subject. So I told him all about it. I said—

"I'll tell you something, but you mustn't speak of it to Mr Carstairs, or father, or anybody; just think over it yourself, and try if you can help her. Rachel knows—she found out for herself, as I did. Vere is not brave nor submissive, nor anything that you think; it is only a pretence, for in reality she is broken-hearted. She won't allow herself to give in like other people, so she has determined to brave it out, and pretend that she doesn't care. She has always been admired and envied, and would hate it if people pitied her now, and I think there is another reason. She is angry! Angry that this should have happened to her, and that it should have happened just now when she was enjoying herself so much, and was so young and pretty. She feels that she has been ill-used, and it makes her cold and bitter. I've felt the same myself when things went wrong. It isn't right, of course: one ought to be sweet and submissive, but—can't you understand?"

"Yes," said Will, quickly. He stopped in his pacings to and fro, and stood thinking it over with his head leant forward on his chest. His face looked so kind, and troubled, and sorry. "Oh, yes," he said, "I understand only too well. Poor girl, poor child! It's awfully sad, for it is going to make it all so much more difficult for her. She doesn't see it, of course, but what she is trying to do is to accept the burden and refuse the consolation which comes with it."

"I must say I fail to see much consolation in an injured spine," I said hastily, and he looked across the room, opening his eyes with that quick, twinkling light which I loved to see.

"Ask Rachel," he said, "ask Rachel! If she broke her back to-morrow she would have at least twenty good reasons for congratulation with which to edify me for the first time we met. Wouldn't you, dear? I am quite sure you would accept it as a blessing in disguise."

"If I broke my back I should die, Will. It is always fatal, I believe!" quoth Rachel the literal, blushing with pleasure at his praise, but talking as primly and properly as if she were addressing a class in a school. She is a queer girl to be engaged to!

I saw Will's eyebrows give just one little twitch on their own account, as if he thought so himself, but the next moment he sat down beside her and said gently —

"But if you were in Miss Sackville's place, how would you feel? How would you face the truth?"

She leant back in her chair and stared before her with big, rapt eyes, her fingers clasping and unclasping themselves on her knee.

"There is only one way — to look to God for help and courage. Pride and anger can never carry her through the long days and nights that will be so hard to bear. They must fail her in the end, and leave her more helpless than before. The consolations are there, if she will open her eyes to see them, and afterwards — afterwards she will have learnt her lesson!"

We sat quiet for quite a long time, and then came the inevitable summons, and Rachel went away and left us alone.

"I told you she was the best woman in the world!" Will said, smiling at me proudly. I didn't feel inclined to smile at all, but the tears came suddenly to my eyes, and I began to sob like a baby.

"Oh, yes, yes, but I am not, and Vere is my sister, and she was so pretty and gay. I can't be resigned for her! I can't bear to see her lying flat on her back; I can't bear to think of that awful chair. How can I talk to her of submission when I'm rebellious myself? I'm all hot, and sore, and miserable, and I want to know why, why, why? Why was our dear old home burnt when other houses are safe and sound? Why should we be crippled and made sad and gloomy just when we thought it was going to be so nice? All my school life I have looked forward to coming home, and now it's all spoiled! I'm not made like Rachel. I can't sit down and be quiet. It doesn't come natural to me to be resigned; I want to argue and understand the meaning of things. I have to fight it through every inch of the way."

"I, too, Babs," he said sadly. "I'm afraid I have kicked very hard against the pricks several times in my life. Every now and then — very rarely — one meets a sweet soul like Rachel who knows nothing of these struggles; they are born saints, and appear to rise superior to temptations, but most of us are continually fighting. There's this consolation, that the hour of victory can never be so sweet as when it comes after a struggle."

"And Vere — will she win too? I can think of no one but her just now. We used often to quarrel, and I've been jealous of her hundreds of times. I never knew I loved her so much till we were in danger, but now I'd give my life to save her, and help her through this terrible time!"

"And you will do it, too. Vere will win her battle, but not with her own weapons, as Rachel says. Pride and anger won't carry her very far down the road she has to travel, poor child. It will be a gentler weapon."

"You mean—?"

Will turned his back to me, and stood staring out of the window. He looked so big and strong himself, as if no weakness could touch him.

"I mean—love," he said softly.

I wondered what he meant. I wondered why he turned his face from me as he spoke. I wondered if the thought of Vere lying there all broken and lovely was too much for his composure, and if he was longing to save her himself. But then there was Rachel. He could never be false to poor trusting Rachel!

Chapter Twelve.

August 20th.

It is lovely to be able to go out again into the sweet summer land, and drive about with father and mother, and have our nice, homely talks again. The Greaves' are perfect angels of kindness, and what we should have done without their hospitality I'm sure I can't tell, but every family has its own little ways, and, of course, you like your own the best. The Greaves' way is always to say exactly precisely whatever they mean and nothing beyond, and to think you rather mad if you do anything else. Our way is to have little jokes and allusions, and a great deal of chatter about nothing in particular, and to think other people bores if they don't do the same. We call our belongings by proper names. My umbrella is "Jane," because she is a plain, domestic-looking creature, and mother's, with the tortoiseshell and gold, is "Mirabella," and our cat is "Miss Davis," after a singing-mistress who squalled, and the new laundry-maid is "Monkey-brand," because she can't wash clothes. It's silly, perhaps, but it *does* help your spirits! When I go out on a wet day and say to my maid "Bring 'Jane,' please," the sight of her face always sends me off in good spirits. She tries so hard not to laugh.

Father and I just make plain, straightforward jokes, like everyone else, but mother jokes daintily, as she does everything else. It's lovely to listen to her when she is in a frisky mood!

We are all depressed enough just now, goodness knows, but it cheers us up a little to be together, and, in comparison with the Greaves' conversation, ours sounds frisky. Yesterday we drove up to see the dear home, at which dozens of men are already at work. It was at once better and worse than I expected. The ivy is still green in places, and they don't think it is all destroyed, so that the first view from the bottom of the drive was a relief. Near at hand we saw the terrible damage done, and, when I went inside for a few minutes, the smell was still so strong that I had to hurry back into the air. It will take months to put things right, and meantime father has taken a furnished house four miles off, where we go as soon as Vere can be moved, and stay until she is strong enough to travel to the sea, or to some warm, sunny place for the winter. We shall probably be away for ages. No balls, Una! No dissipations, and partners, and admiration, and pretty new frocks, as you expected. Furnished houses and hospital nurses, and a long, anxious illness to watch. Those are your portion, my dear!

I am a wretch to think of myself at all. Rachel wouldn't; but I do, and it's no use pretending I don't. I'm horribly, horribly disappointed! One part of me feels cross and injured; the other part of me longs to be good and unselfish, and to cheer and help the others. I haven't had far to look for my sister. While I was searching the neighbourhood for someone to befriend, the opportunity was preparing inside our very own walls! Now then, Una Sackville, brace up! Show what you are made of! You are fond enough of talking— now let us see what you can do!

August 28th.

The spinal chair arrived yesterday when I was at the Lodge. Father cried when he saw it. I hate to see a man cry, and got out of the way as soon as possible, and, when I came back, mother and he were sitting hand in hand in the little parlour, looking quite calm, and kind of sadly happy. I think bearing things together has brought them nearer than they have been for years, so they certainly have found their compensation.

The doctor says Vere is to live out of doors, so this morning she was carried out on her mattress, laid flat on the chair, and wheeled to a corner of the lawn. As I had prophesied, she arranged all details herself. She wore a soft, white serge dressing-gown sort of arrangement, which was loose and comfortable, and a long lace scarf put loosely over her head, and tied under the chin, instead of a hat. Everything was as simple as it could be. Vere had too much good taste to choose unsuitable fineries, but, as she lay with the sunlight flickering down at her beneath the screen of leaves, she looked so touchingly frail and lovely that it broke your heart to see her. Her hair lay in little gold rings on her forehead, the face inside the lace hood had shrunk to such a tiny oval. One had not realised, seeing her in bed, how thin she had grown during these last few weeks!

We all waited on her hand and foot, and walked in procession beside her, gulping hard, and blinking our eyes to keep back the tears whenever we had a quiet chance, and she laughed and admired the trees, and said really it was the quaintest sensation staring straight up at the sky; she felt just like "Johnny Head in Air" in the dear old picture-book! It was a delightful couch—most comfortable! What a lazy summer she should have! If there was one thing she loved more than another, it was having meals in the open air—all in the same high, artificial note which she had used ever since her accident.

We all agreed and gushed, and said, "Yes, darling," "Isn't it, darling?" "So you shall, darling," and we had tea under a big beech-tree, and anyone might have thought we were quite jolly; but I could see father's lip quiver under his moustache, and mother looked old. I hate to see mother look old!

Just as we had finished tea a servant came up to tell father that Will and Mr Carstairs had called to see him. They had too much good feeling to join us where we were, but Vere lifted her languid eyes and said "Stupid men! What are they afraid of? Tell them to come here at once." And no one dared to oppose her.

I shall never forget that scene. It was like treading on sacred ground to be there when Mr Carstairs went forward to take Vere's hand, yet, of course, it would not have done to leave them alone. His face was set, poor fellow, and he couldn't speak. I could see the pulse above his ear beating like a hammer, and was terrified lest he should break down altogether. Vere would never have forgiven that! She thanked him in her pretty society way for all his "favaws," the flowers, and the books, and the letters, all "so amusing, don't you know!" (as if his poor letters could have been amusing!) and behaved really and truly as if they had just met in a ball-room, after an ordinary separation.

"It's quite an age since I saw you; and now, I suppose, it is a case of 'How do you do, and good-bye,'" she said lightly. "You must be longing to get away from this dull place, to pay some of your postponed visits."

"They will have to be postponed a little longer. Dudley is good enough to say he can put me up another week or two, and I should like to see you settled at Bylands. There—there might be something I could do for you," returned the poor man wistfully, but she would not acknowledge any need of help.

"Dearie me! Have you turned furniture remover? Are you proposing to pack me with the rest of our belongings?" she cried, lifting her chin about a quarter of an inch in feeble imitation of her old scornful tilt. It was very pitiful to see her do it, and Mr Carstairs' lip twitched again, and he turned and began talking to mother, leaving the coast clear for Will Dudley. He looked flushed, but his eyes were curiously bright and determined.

"I am so thankful to see you out again, Miss Sackville," he said. "That's the first step forward in your convalescence, and I hope the others may follow quickly!"

That was his cue! He was not going to allow Vere to ignore her illness talking to him; he had determined to make her face it naturally and simply, but the flash in her eyes showed that it would not be too easy. She stared up into his face with a look of cold displeasure, and he stared straight back and said—

"Are you as comfortable as possible? I think that light is rather dazzling to your eyes. Let me move you just a few inches."

"I am perfectly happy, thank you. Pray don't trouble. I prefer to stay where I am."

"I'll move you back again if you don't like it," he said coolly. "There! Now that branch screens you nicely. The sun has moved since you first came out, I expect. Confess, now, that is more comfortable!"

She would not confess, and she could not deny, so she simply dropped her eyelids and refused to answer; but a little thing like that would not daunt Will Dudley, and he went on talking as if she had thanked him as graciously as possible. Presently, however, the hospital nurse gave us a private signal that Vere was getting tired and ought to rest, so we all strolled away and left them alone together beneath the tree.

We had only three days more at the Grange, and during them Rachel devoted herself as much as possible to Vere, trotting between the house and the beech-trees on everlasting missions, and reading aloud for hours together from stupid novels, which I am sure bored her to extinction. Vere herself did not seem to listen very attentively, but I think the sweet, rather monotonous voice had a soothing effect on her nerves; she was relieved to be spared talking, and also intent on studying this strange specimen of human nature.

"Oh, admirable but dullest of Rachels, she absolutely delights in doing what she dislikes! It was as good as a play to watch her face yesterday while she read aloud the reflections of the worldly Lady Peggy! They evidently gave her nerves a severe shock, but as for omitting a passage, as for even skipping an objectionable word, no! not if her life depended upon it. 'It is my duty, and I will.' That is her motto in life. How boring people are who do their duty!" drawled Vere languidly on the last afternoon, as poor Rachel left her to go back to the other invalid, who was no doubt growling like a bear in his den as he waited for her return. Everyone seemed to take Rachel's help for granted, and to think it superfluous to thank her. Even Will himself is far less attentive to her wants than my *fiancé* shall be when I have one. I simply couldn't stand being treated like a favourite aunt, and really and truly he behaves far more as if she were that, than his future wife. He is never in the least tiny bit excited or agitated about seeing her.

I wouldn't admit this to Vere for a thousand pounds, but I felt cross all the same, and said snappishly—

"It's a pity she wasted her time, since you were only jeering at her for her pains. I don't know about enjoying what she hates, but she certainly loves trying to help other people, and I admire her for it. I wish to goodness I were like her!"

At this she smiled more provokingly than ever.

"Yes. I've noticed the imitation. It's amusing. All the more so that it is so poor a success. Your temper is not of the quality to be kept persistently in the background, my dear."

It isn't. But I *had* tried hard to keep patient and gentle the last few weeks, even when Vere aggravated me most. I had been so achingly sorry for her that I would have cut off my right hand to help her, so it hurt when she gibed at me like that.

"I'm sorry I was impatient! I wanted so badly to help you, dear. You must forgive me if I was cross."

"Babs, *don't!*" she gasped, and her face was convulsed with emotion. For one breathless moment, as we clutched hands and drew close together, I thought the breakdown had come at last, but she fought down her sobs, crying in tones of piteous entreaty—

"Don't let me cry! Stop me! Oh, Babs, don't let me do it. If I once begin I can never stop!"

"But wouldn't it be a relief to you, darling? Everyone has been terrified lest you were putting too great a strain on yourself. If you gave way once to me—it doesn't matter for me—it might do you good. Cry, darling, if you want, and I'll cry with you!"

But she protested more vigorously than ever. "No, no, I daren't! I can't face it! Be cross with me—be neglectful—leave me to myself, but for pity's sake don't be so patient, Babs! It makes me silly, and I must keep up, whatever happens. Say something now to make me stop—quickly!"

"I expect the men will be here any moment. You'll look hideous with red eyes," I said gruffly. It was the only thing I could think of, and perhaps it did as well as anything else, for she calmed down by degrees, and there was no more sign of a breakdown that night.

After that day we seemed to understand each other better, and when I saw danger signals I was snappy on purpose, and felt like a martyr when Will and Mr Carstairs glared at me, and thought what a wretch I was. We wanted Vere to be resigned and natural about her illness, but we dreaded and feared a hysterical breakdown, which must leave her weaker than ever, and she had said herself that if she once began to cry she could never leave off.

Chapter Thirteen.

September 5th.

Four days later we left the Grange and came to our new home, a furnished house four miles away. It is a big, square, prosaic-looking building, but comfortable, with a nice big garden, so we are fortunate to have found such a place in the neighbourhood. We told each other gushingly how fortunate we had been, every time that we discovered anything that we hated more than usual, and were obtrusively gay all that first horrid evening.

Vere's two rooms had been made home-like and pretty with treasures saved from the Moat, and new curtains and cushions and odds and ends like that; but we left the other rooms as they were, and pretended that we liked sitting on crimson satin chairs with gold legs. Father is lost without his nice gunny, sporty sanctum. Mother looks pathetically out of place in the bald, ugly rooms, and I feel a pelican in the wilderness without my belongings but when you have come through great big troubles you are ashamed to fuss over little things like these.

Also, to tell the truth, we are thankful to be together in a place of our own again. Mrs Greaves and Rachel had been sweet to us, but they had one invalid on their hands already, and we could not help feeling that we gave a great deal of trouble. They said they were sorry to lose us, and that we had been an interest in their quiet lives, and I do think that was true. Vere, with her beauty and her tragedy, her lovely clothes and dainty ways, was as good as a three-volume novel to people who wear blue serge the whole year round, do their hair neatly in knobs like walnuts, and never indulge in anything more exciting than a garden party. Then there was the romantic figure of poor Jim Carstairs hovering in the background, ready at any moment to do desperate deeds, if thereby he could win a smile of approval, so different from that other complacent lover, who was "content to wait" and never knew the semblance of a qualm! I used to watch Rachel watch Jim, and thought somehow that she felt the difference, and was not so serene as she had been when I first knew her. Her face looked sad sometimes, but not for long, for she had so little time to think of herself. I agree with Will that she is the best woman in the world, and the sweetest and most unselfish.

The house where Will lives is nearer "The Clift" than the old home, and the two men come over often to see us. They had reconnoitred the grounds before we arrived, and knew just the nicest portions for Vere's chair for each part of the day, and Jim had noticed how she started at the sudden appearance of a newcomer, and had hit on a clever way of giving her warning of an approach. Lying quite flat as she does, with her face turned stiffly upwards, it had been impossible to see anyone till he was close at hand, but now he has suspended a slip of mirror from the branches of the favourite trees in such a position that they reflect the whole stretch of lawn. It is quite pretty to look up and see the figures moving about; the maids bringing out tea, or father playing with the dogs. Vere can even watch a game of tennis or croquet without turning her head. We were all delighted, and gushed with admiration at his ingenuity, and Vere said, "Thank you, Jim," and smiled at him, and that was worth all the praise in the world.

He told us that he was going home at the end of the week, and one day I listened to a conversation which I never should have heard, but it wasn't my fault. Vere and I were alone, and when we saw Jim coming she got into a state of excitement, and made me vow and declare that I would not leave her. I couldn't possibly refuse, for she isn't allowed to be excited, but I twisted my chair as far away as I dared, humped up my shoulders and buried myself in my book. Jim knew I would do my best for him, but it's disgusting how difficult it is to fix your attention on one thing, and close your ears to something still more interesting. I honestly did try, and the jargon that the book and the conversation made together was something too ridiculous. It was like this—

"Maud was sitting gazing out of the window at the unending stream of traffic." "This is our last talk! I told Dudley not to come, for there's so much to say." "It was her first visit to London, and to the innocent country mind—" "Don't put me off, dear! I must speak to-day, or wait here till I do." "Innocent country mind—innocent country mind." "No matter if it does pain me. I will take the risk. I just wish you to know." "Innocent country mind it seemed as if—" But it was no use; my eyes travelled steadily down the page, but to this moment I can't tell you what Maud's innocent country mind made of it. I could hear nothing but Jim's deep, earnest voice.

"I don't ask anything from you. You never encouraged me when you were well, and I won't take advantage of your weakness. I just want you to realise that I am yours, as absolutely and truly as though we were formally engaged. You are free as air to do in every respect as you will, but you cannot alter my position. I cannot alter it myself. The thing has grown beyond my control. You are my life; for weal or woe I must be faithful to you. I make only one claim—that when you need a friend you will send for me. When there is any service, however small, which I can render, you will let me do it. It isn't much to ask, is it, sweetheart?"

There was a moment's pause—I tried desperately and unsuccessfully to get interested in Maud, and then Vere's voice said gently—more gently than I had ever heard her speak—

"Dear old Jim, you are so good always! It's a very unfair arrangement, and it would be horribly selfish to agree. I'd like well enough to have you coming down; it would be a distraction, and help to pass the time. I expect we shall be terribly quiet here, and I have always been accustomed to having some man to fly round and wait upon me. There is no one I would like better than you—wait a moment—no one I would like better while I am ill! I can trust you, and you are so thoughtful and kind. But if I get well again? What then? It is best to be honest, isn't it, Jim? You used to bore me sometimes when I was well, and you might bore me again. It isn't fair!"

"It is perfectly fair, for I am asking no promises. If I can be of the least use or comfort to you now, that is all I ask. I know I am a dull, heavy fellow. It isn't likely you could be bothered with me when you were well."

Silence. I would not look, but I could imagine how they looked. Jim bending over her with his strong brown features a-quiver with emotion. Vere with the lace scarf tied under her chin, her lovely white little face gazing up at him in unwonted gentleness.

"I wonder," she said slowly, "I wonder what there is in me to attract you, Jim! You are not like other men. You would not care for appearances only, yet, apart from my face and figure—my poor figure of which I was so proud—there is nothing left which could really please you. I have been a vain, empty-headed girl all my life. I cared for myself more than anything on earth. I do now! You think I am brave and uncomplaining, but it is all a sham. I am too proud to whine, but in reality I am seething with bitterness and rebellion. I am longing to get well, not to lead a self-sacrificing life like Rachel Greaves, but to feel fit again, and wear pretty clothes, and dance, and flirt, and be admired—that's what I want most, Jim; that's *all* I want!"

He put out his hands and took hers. I don't know how I knew it, but I did, though Maud was still staring out of the window, and I was still staring at Maud.

"Poor darling!" he said huskily. "Poor darling!"

He didn't preach a bit, though it was a splendid opening if he had wanted one, but I think the sorrow and regret in his voice was better than words. Vere knew what he meant, and why he was sorry. I heard a little gasping sound, and then a rapid, broken whispering.

"I know—I know! I ought to feel differently! Sometimes in the night—oh, the long, long nights, Jim!—the pain is so bad, and it seems as if light would never come, and I lie awake staring into the darkness, and a fear comes over me... I feel all alone in a new world that is strange and terrible, where the things I cared for most don't matter at all, and the things I neglected take up all the room. And I'm frightened, Jim! I'm frightened! I've lost my footing, and it's all blackness and confusion. Is it because I am so wicked that I am afraid to be alone with my thoughts? I was so well and strong before this. I slept so soundly that I never seemed to have time to think."

"Perhaps that's the reason of it, sweetheart. You needed the time, and it has been given to you this way, and when you have found yourself the need will be over, and you will be well again."

"Found myself!" she repeated musingly. "Is there a real self that I know nothing of hidden away somewhere? That must be the self you care for, Jim. Tell me! I want to know—what is there in me which made you care so much? You acknowledge that I am vain?"

"Y–es!"

"And selfish?"

He wouldn't say "Yes," and couldn't deny it, so just sat silently and refused to answer.

"And a flirt?"

"Yes."

"And very cruel to you sometimes, Jim?" said Vere in that new, sweet, gentle voice.

"You didn't mean it, darling. It was only thoughtlessness."

"No, no! I did mean it! It was dreadful of me, but I liked to experiment and feel my power. You had better know the truth once for all; it will help you to forget all about such a wretched girl."

"Nothing can make me forget. You could tell me what you like about yourself, it would make no difference; I am past all that. You are the one woman in the world for me. At first it was your beauty which attracted me, but that stage was over long ago. It makes no difference to me now how you look. Nothing makes any difference. If you were never to leave that couch—"

But she called out at that, interrupting him sharply—

"Don't say it! Don't suggest for a moment that it is possible! Oh, Jim, you don't believe it! You don't really think I could be like this all my life? I will be very good, and do all they say, and keep quiet and not excite myself. I will do anything—anything—but I must get better in the end! I could not bear a life like this!"

"The doctors all tell us you will recover in time, darling, but it's a terribly hard waiting. I wish I could bear the pain for you; but you will let me do what I can, won't you, Vere? I am a dull stick. No one knows it better than I do myself, but make use of me just now; let me fetch and carry for you; let me run down every few weeks to see you, and give you the news. It will bind you to nothing in the future. Whatever happens, I should be grateful to you all my life for giving me so much happiness."

"Dear old Jim! You are too good for me. How could I possibly say 'No' to such a request?" sighed Vere softly. I think she was very nearly crying just then, but I made another desperate effort to interest myself in Maud, and soon afterwards he went away.

Vere looked at me curiously when I returned to the seat by her side, and I told her the truth.

"I tried to read, I did, honestly, but I heard a good deal! It was your own fault. You wouldn't let me go away."

"Then you know something you may not have known before—how a good man can love! I have treated Jim Carstairs like a dog, and this is how he behaves in return. I don't deserve such devotion."

"Nobody does. But I envy you, Vere. I envy you even now, with all your pain. It must be the best thing in the world to be loved like that."

"Sentimental child!" she said, smiling; but it was a real smile, not a sneer; and when mother came up a few minutes later, Vere looked at her anxiously, noticing for the very first time how ill and worn she looked.

"You looked fagged, mother dear. Do sit still and rest," she said, in her old, caressing manner. Mother flushed, and looked ten years younger on the spot.

Chapter Fourteen.

September 20th.

I expected Vere to be quite different after this—to give up being cold and defiant, and be her own old self. I thought it was a kind of crisis, and that she would go on getting better and better—morally, I mean. But she doesn't! At least, if she does, it is only by fits and starts. Sometimes she is quite angelic for a whole day, and the next morning is so crotchety and aggravating that it nearly drives one wild. I suppose no one gets patient and long-suffering all at once; it is like convalescence after an illness—up and down, up and down, all the time; but it's disappointing to the nurses. She does try, poor dear, but it must be difficult to go on trying when one day is exactly like the last, and you do nothing but lie still, and your back aches, aches, aches. Jim is not always present to lavish his devotion upon her, and now that the first agitation is over we onlookers are getting used to seeing her ill, and are less frantically attentive than at first, which, of course, must be trying, too; but one cannot always live at high pressure. I believe one would get callous about earthquakes if they only happened often enough.

Summer is passing away and autumn coming on, and it grows damp and mouldy, and we have to sit indoors for most of the day. When I have any time to think of myself I feel so tired; and one day Vere said abruptly—

"Babs, you are thin! Upon my word, child, I can see your cheek-bones. What have you been doing to yourself?"

Thin! Blessed word! I leapt from my seat and rushed to the nearest glass, and it was true! I stared, and stared, and wondered where my eyes had been these last weeks. My cheeks had sunk till they were oval instead of round. I looked altogether about half the old size. What would the girls say if they could behold their old "Circle" now? It used to be my ambition to be described as a "tall, slim girl," and now I turned, and twisted, and attitudinised before that glass,

94

and, honestly, that was just exactly what I looked! I took hold of my dress, and it bagged! I put my fingers inside my belt, and the whole hand slipped through! My face of rapture made Vere laugh with almost the old trill.

"You goose! You look as if you had come into a fortune! I don't deny that it is an improvement, but you mustn't overdo it. It would be too hard luck for mother if we were both ill at the same time. All this anxiety has been too much for you. I had better turn nurse, and let you be patient for a little time, and I'll prescribe a little change and excitement. Firstly, a becoming new toilette for dinner to-night, in which you can do justice to your charms."

Vere never dines with us now, as the evenings are her worst time, and she spends them entirely in her own little sitting-room. I am always with her to read aloud, or play games, or talk, just as she prefers; but this night there were actually some people coming to dinner for the first time since the pre-historic ages before the fire. The people around had been very kind and attentive, and mother thought it our duty to ask a few of them; so four couples were coming, and Will Dudley to pair with me. It was quite an excitement after our quiet days; and Vere called her maid, and sent her to bring down one or two evening dresses which had been rescued uninjured from a hanging cupboard and left untouched until now in the box in which they had been packed.

"Miss Una is so much thinner, I believe she could get into them now, Terese; and I have a fancy to dress her up to-night and see what we can make of her," she said, smiling; and Terese beamed with delight, not so much at the thought of dressing me, as in joy at hearing her beloved mistress take an interest in anything again. She adores Vere, as all servants do. It's because she makes pretty speeches to them and praises them when they do things well, instead of treating them like machines, as most people do. In my superior moments I used to think that she was hypocritical, while I myself was honest and outspoken; but I am beginning to see that praise is sometimes more powerful than blame. I am really becoming awfully grown-up and judicious. I hardly know myself sometimes.

Well, Terese brought in three dresses, and I tried them on in succession, and Vere decided which was most becoming, and directed little alterations, and said what flowers I was to wear, and how my hair was to be done, just exactly as if I were a new doll which made an amusing plaything. I had to be dressed in her room, too, and she lay watching me with her big wan eyes, issuing directions to Terese, and saying pretty things to me. It was one of her very, very nicest days, and I did love her.

When the last touch was given I surveyed myself in the long mirror and "blushed at my own reflection," like the girl in books who is going to her first ball. I really did look my very, very nicest, and so grown up, and sort of fragile and interesting, instead of the big, hulking schoolgirl of a year ago. The lovely moonshiny dress would have suited anyone, and Terese had made my hair look just about twice as thick as when I do it myself. I can't think how she manages! I did feel pleased, and thought it sweet of Vere to be pleased too, for it was not in girl nature to avoid feeling lone and lorn at being left alone, stretched on that horrid couch. She tried to smile bravely as I left her to go downstairs, but her lips trembled a little, and she said in a wistful way—

"Perhaps, if I feel well enough, you might bring Mr Dudley up to see me for a few minutes after dinner. Terese will let you know how I am."

I had to promise, of course, but I didn't like doing it. It didn't seem fair either to Rachel or to Jim Carstairs to let these two see too much of each other, or to Vere herself, for that matter; for I always have a kind of dread that this time it may not be all pretence on her side. She seems a little different when Will is there, less absolutely confident and sure of herself.

The four couples arrived in good time. How uninteresting middle-aged couples are! One always wondered why they married each other, for they seem so prosy and matter-of-fact. When I am a middle-aged couple, or half of one, I shall be like father and mother, and carry about with me the breath of eternal romance, as Lorna would say, and I shall "Bant," and never allow myself to grow stout, and simply annihilate my husband if he dares to call me "my dear." Fancy coming down to being a "my dear" in a cap!

I had gone into the conservatory to show some plants to funny old bald Mr Farrer, and when he toddled out to show a bloom to his wife I came face to face with Will, standing in the entrance by himself, looking so handsome and bored. He gave a quick step forward as he saw me and exclaimed first "Babs!" and then, with a sudden change of voice and manner, almost as if he were startled—

"Una!"

He didn't shake hands with me, and I felt a little bit scared and shy, for it is only very, very rarely that he calls me by my name, and I have a kind of feeling that when he does he likes me more than usual. It was Vere's dress, of course; perhaps it made me look like her. We went back into the drawing-room, and stood in a corner like dummies until dinner was announced.

I thought it would have been such fun, but it wasn't. Will was dull and distrait, and he hardly looked at me once, and talked about sensible impersonal things the whole time. Of course, I like sensible conversation; one feels humiliated if a man does nothing but frivol, but there is a happy medium. When you are nineteen and looking your best, you don't care to be treated as if you were a hundred and fifty, and a fright at that. Will and I have always been good friends, and being engaged as he is, I expect him to be perfectly frank and out-spoken.

I tried to be lively and keep the conversation going, but it was such an effort that I grew tired, and I really think I am rather delicate for once in my life, for what with the exertion and the depression, I felt quite ill by the time dessert was on the table. All the ladies said how pale I was in the drawing-room, and mother puckered her eyebrows when she looked at me. Dear, sweet mother! It was horrid of me to be pleased at anything which worried her, but when you have been of no account, and all the attention has been lavished on someone else, it is really rather soothing to have people think of you for a change.

Terese met me coming out of the dining-room, and said that Vere was well enough to see Mr Dudley, so I took him upstairs as soon as he appeared. Passing through the hall, I saw a letter addressed to me in Lorna's handwriting, on the table, and carried it up with me to read while they were talking. They wouldn't want me, and it would be a comfort to remember that Lorna did. I was just in the mood to be a martyr, so when I had seen Will seated beside the couch, and noticed that Vere had been arrayed for the occasion in her prettiest wrap, with frilled cushion covers to match, I went right off to the end of the room and sat down on the most uncomfortable chair I could find. When one feels low it is comical what a relief it is to punish oneself still further. When I thought myself ill-used as a child, I used always to refuse tart and cream, which I loved, and eat rice pudding, which I hated. The uncomfortable chair was the rice pudding in this instance, but I soon forgot all about it, and even about Vere and Will, in the excitement of reading that letter.

"My own Maggie,—(on the second day after we met at school Lorna and I decided to call each other 'Maggie'— short for 'magnetic attraction'—but we only do it when we write, otherwise it excites curiosity, and that is horrid in matters of the heart!)—My own Maggie,—It is ages since I heard from you, darling. Why didn't you answer my letter last week? But I know how occupied you are, poor angel, and won't scold you as you deserve. I think of you every moment of the day, and do so long to be able to help you to bear your heavy burden. How little we thought when you went home how soon the smiling future would turn into a frown! We both seem to have left our careless youth far behind, for I have my own trials too, though nothing to yours, my precious darling.

"I have heaps to tell you. I decided to have the blue dress, after all, and the dressmaker has made it sweetly, with dozens of little tucks. I wore it at an afternoon 'At Home' yesterday, and it looked lovely. Lots of people were there. Wallace took me. He is at home helping with the practice. Maggie, my darling, I am really writing to ask you the most awful favour. Would you, could you, come down to stay with us for a few weeks? I do long for you so. There is no one on earth but you to whom I can speak my utmost thoughts, and I feel all bottled up, for there are some things one can't write. I know you feel this, too, dearest, for there is a change in the tone of your letters, and I read between the lines that you have lots to tell me. We could have great sport with Wallace to take us about, and the people around are very hospitable, and always ask us out when we have a visitor. Wallace saw your photograph one day, and said you were 'ripping,' and he is quite keen on your coming, though, as a rule, he doesn't care for girls. Mother will write to Mrs Sackville if you think there is the slightest chance that you can be spared. Of course, darling, if you feel it your duty to stay at home I won't persuade you to come. You remember how we vowed to urge each other to do our best and noblest, but perhaps if you had a little change you would go back refreshed and able to help your people better than you can at present. Anyway, write soon, darling, and put me out of my suspense. I sha'n't sleep a wink till I hear. Oh, the bliss of having you all to myself! How we would talk!

"Your own Maggie."

Yes, it would indeed be bliss! I longed for Lorna, but it did not seem possible to go away and enjoy myself, and leave Vere so helpless and sad. I decided not to say a word about the invitation, but I couldn't help thinking about it. Lorna lived in a big town house in the middle of a street; her father is a busy doctor, and is not at all rich, but very jolly. She is the only unmarried girl, and has half-a-dozen brothers in all stages, from twelve up to Wallace, who is a doctor, and thinks my photograph is "ripping!" It all seemed so tempting, and so refreshingly different from anything I have known. I began imagining it all—the journey, meeting Lorna at the station, and tearing about with all those funny, merry boys, instead of tiptoeing about a sick-room; Wallace being nice and attentive to me, instead of in love with someone else, as all the men at home seem to be, and Lorna creeping into my bed at night, with her hair in a funny, tight little pigtail, and talking, talking, talking for hour after hour. Oh, I did want to go so badly! The tears came to my eyes for very longing. My resolution did not waver one bit, but I was dreadfully sorry for myself, all the same.

Suddenly I became aware that there was a dead silence in the room. How long it had lasted I can't tell, but when I looked up there were Vere and Will staring at me, and looking as if they had been staring for an age, and couldn't understand what on earth was the matter. I jumped and got red, and blinked away the tears, and Vere said—

"What is the matter, child? Have you had bad news? You look as if your heart was broken!"

"Oh, no—there's no news at all. I am tired, I think, and stupid, and wasn't thinking of what I was doing."

"You seemed to be thinking of something pretty deeply; and what business have you to be tired—a baby like you? I have been prescribing for her to-day, Mr Dudley. Have you noticed how thin she has grown? She hadn't discovered it herself until I told her, wonderful to relate."

"I don't think she has thought of herself at all these last few months," said Will, quietly.

He only just gave one glance at me, and then looked away, and I was thankful, for every drop of blood in my body seemed to fly to my face in the joy of hearing him praise me like that. Vere did not speak for a moment or two, and then she just asked who the letter was from.

"Lorna Forbes. She writes every week. I haven't written to her for an age—nearly a month."

They both knew about Lorna, and teased me about her when I quoted her opinion, and now, to my surprise, Will lifted his eyes from the carpet, and said, looking me full in the face—

"And she wants you to pay her a visit, and you think you ought not to go?"

How could he guess? I was so taken aback that at first I could only gasp and stare.

"How in the world did you know?" I asked at last, and he smiled and said—

"Your face was very eloquent. It was very easy to read, wasn't it, Miss Sackville?"

"I did not find it so transparent as you seem to have done; I suppose I am dense," Vere replied, with a laugh that sounded a little bit strained. "Is it true, Babs? Has Mr Dudley read the signs correctly?"

I had to confess, making as light of it as possible, but they weren't deceived a bit.

"You hardly looked as if you didn't 'care,'" Will remarked drily, and Vere said quite quickly and eagerly—

"You must go, Babs—of course you must go! It is the very thing you need. You have been a ministering angel to me, and I'm very grateful, but I don't want the responsibility of making you ill. Change and the beloved Lorna will soon bring back your roses, and it will be amusing to hear of your escapades when you return. Don't think of me! It is good for me to be quiet, and there are plenty of friends who will come in for an hour or two if I feel the need of society. You will take pity on me, won't you, Mr Dudley? You will come sometimes and have tea with mother and me?"

"I shall be delighted," said Will, gravely. As for me, I didn't know whether to be most pleased or depressed. I should pay my visit to

Lorna, that was practically settled from the moment Vere approved of the proposal, which was one nice thing; and another was her remark that I had been an angel; but it seemed as if I could be very easily spared, and I had grown to think myself indispensable these last few weeks. We talked a little more about it, and then Will and I went downstairs. He didn't speak until we were nearly at the drawing-room door, when he said abruptly—

"You are very eager to get away! Are you so tired of this neighbourhood and all the people it contains?"

"Oh, so tired! so utterly, utterly tired!" I cried earnestly.

It sounded rude, perhaps, but at the moment I really felt it. I had reached the stage of tiredness when I had a perfect craving for a change. He didn't say a word, but stalked straight forward, and never spoke to me again except to say good-night. It doesn't concern me, of course, but I do hope for Rachel's sake that he hasn't a sulky nature.

Heigh-ho for Lorna! I am going at the end of next week. I am positively bursting with delight!

Chapter Fifteen.

October 4th.

Here I am! It is not a bit as I imagined, but ever so much nicer. Lorna looks sweet in grown-up things, and she thinks I look sweet in mine. She comes into my bed at nights, and we talk for hours. The house is right in the middle of the town, in a dingy old square, where the trees look more black than green. It is ugly and shabby, but there is plenty of room, which is a good thing, for I am sure it is needed. The doctor sits in his consulting-room all the morning seeing patients, who wait their turn in the dining-room, and if there are a great many you have to be late for lunch, but, as Lorna says, "That means another guinea, so we mustn't grumble!" They are not at all rich, because the six boys cost so much to educate. They are all away at school and college, except the oldest and the youngest, of whom more anon.

Dr Forbes is an old love. He has shaggy grey hair, and merry eyes, and the funniest way of talking aloud to himself without knowing what he is saying. At lunch he will keep up a running conversation like this: "Nasty case—yes, nasty case! Poor woman, poor woman! Very little chance—little chance—Very good steak, my dear—an admirable dinner you have given me! Am-pu-ta-tion at eleven— mustn't forget the medicine. Three times a day. A little custard, if you please," and so on, and so on, and the others never take any notice, but eat away as if no one were speaking.

Mrs Forbes is large and kind, and shakes when she laughs. I don't think she is clever, exactly, but she's an admirable mother, and lets them do exactly as they like.

Wallace isn't bad. He is twenty-four, and fairly good-looking, and not as conceited as men generally are at that age. Personally, I prefer them older, but he evidently approves of me, and that is soothing to the feelings. Julias, surnamed "Midas," is only twelve, and a most amusing character. I asked Lorna and Wallace how he got his nickname, as we sat together over a fire in the old schoolroom the first night. They laughed, and Wallace said — (of course, I call him Dr Wallace, really, but I can't be bothered to write it here) —

"Because everything he touches turns to gold, or, to speak more correctly, copper! He has a genius for accumulating money, and has what we consider quite a vast sum deposited in the savings bank. My father expects him to develop into a great financier, and we hope he may pension off all his brothers and sister, to keep them from the workhouse. To do Midas justice, he is not mean in a good cause, and I believe he will do the straight thing."

"But how can he make money? He is only twelve. I don't see how it is to be done," I cried. And they laughed and said —

"It began years ago — when he shed his front teeth. Mother used to offer us sixpence a tooth when they grew waggly, and we pulled them out without any fuss. We each earned sixpences in our turn, and all went well; but when Midas once began he was not content to stop, and worked away at sound, new double teeth, until he actually got out two in one afternoon. Then mother took alarm, and the pay was stopped. There was an interregnum after that, and what came next? Let me see — it must have been the sleeping sickness. Midas grew very rapidly, Miss Sackville, and it was very difficult to get him to bed at nights, so as the mater thought he was suffering from the want of sleep, she promised him threepence an hour for every hour he spent in bed before nine o'clock. After that he retired regularly every night at seven, and on half-holidays it's a solemn fact that he was in bed at four o'clock, issuing instructions as to the viands which were to be brought up for his refreshment! The mater stood it for a time, but the family finances wouldn't bear the strain, so she limited the hours and reduced the fee, and Midas returned to his old ways. What came after that, Lorna?"

"I don't know — I forget! Of course there was Biggs —"

"Ah, yes, Miss Biggs! Miss Biggs, you must know, Miss Sackville, is an ancient friend of the family, whom we consider it a duty to invite for a yearly visit. She is an admirable old soul, but very deaf, very slow, and incredibly boring. Her favourite occupation is to bring down sheaves of letters from other maiden ladies, and insist upon reading them aloud to the assembled family. 'I have just had a letter from Louisa Gibbings; I am sure you will like to hear it,' she will say calmly, when the poor old parents are enjoying a quiet read after dinner, and we youngsters are in the middle of a game. None of us have the remotest idea who Louisa Gibbings may be, and don't want to know, but we are bound to listen to three sheets of uninteresting information as to how 'My brother in China contemplates a visit home next year.' 'My garden is looking charming, but the peas are very poor this season.' 'You will be grieved to hear that our good Mary still suffers acutely from the old complaint,' etcetera, etcetera, etcetera. Last time she paid her visit when Midas had his Easter holidays, and one day, seeing mother quite exhausted by her efforts at entertainment, he made the brilliant proposal that he should take Miss Biggs off her hands for the sum of fourpence an hour. Mother agreed with enthusiasm, and Midas made quite a fortune in the next fortnight, with equal satisfaction to all concerned. In the morning he took Miss Biggs out walking to see the sights, and gave her his advice in the purchase of new caps. In the afternoon the wily young wretch cajoled her into giving him an hour's coaching in French, and in the evening he challenged her to draughts and dominoes, and made a point of allowing her to win. Mother had a chance of attending to her work; father could read in peace; Midas was in a condition of such complacent good nature that he declared Miss Biggs was a 'ripping old girl,' and she on her part gave him the credit for being 'the most gentlemanly youth she had ever encountered.' I believe she is really attached to him, and should not wonder if she remembers him substantially in her will. Then Midas will have scored a double triumph!"

Wallace and Lorna laughed as heartily as I did over these histories. They really are a most good-natured family, and Wallace treats Lorna as politely as if she were someone else, and not his own sister, which is very different from some young men I could mention. I had put on my blue dress, and I knew quite well that he admired it and me, and that put me in such good spirits that I was quite sparkling and witty. He stayed talking to us until after nine, when he had to go downstairs to write some letters.

"Thank goodness! I thought he would never go. What a bore he is!" Lorna said, when the door closed behind him.

I didn't feel like that at all, but I disguised my feelings, and told her the details and the adventures of the last three months, and about Vere, and the house, and my own private tribulations, and she sympathised and looked at everything from my point of view, in the nice, unprejudiced way friends have. It was very soothing, and I could have gone on for a long time, but it was only polite to return the compliment, so I said—

"Now we must talk about you! You said in your last letter that you had many troubles of which you could not write. Poor, sweet thing, tell me about them! Begin at the beginning. What do you consider your very greatest trial?"

Lorna pondered. She is dark and slight, and wears her hair parted in the middle, and puffed out at the sides in a quaint fashion that just suits her style. She wrinkled her brows, and stared into space in a rapt, melancholy fashion.

"I think," she said, slowly, at last, "I think it is the drawing-room!"

I was surprised, but still not surprised, for the drawing-room is awful! Big and square, and filled with heavy furniture, and a perfect shopful of ugly ornaments and bead mats, and little tables, and milking-stools, and tambourines, and bannerettes, and all the kind of things that were considered lovely ages ago, but which no self-respecting girl of our age could possibly endure. Lorna told me thrilling tales of her experience with that room.

"When I first came home, mother saw that I didn't like it, so she said she knew quite well that she was old-fashioned and behind the times, and now that she had a grown-up daughter she would leave the arrangement of such things to her, and I could alter the room as much as ever I liked. So, my dear, I made Mary bring the biggest tray in the house, and I filled it three times over with gimcracks of all descriptions, and sent them up to the box-room cupboard. I kept about three tables instead of seven, with really nice things on them, and left a good sweep of floor on which you could walk about without knocking things down. I pulled out the piano from the wall, and lowered the pictures, and gathered all the old china together, and put it on the chimney-piece, and—and—oh, I can't tell you all the alterations, but you would hardly have known it for the same room! It looked quite decent. When all was finished, I sent for mother, and she came in and sat down, and, my dear, she turned quite white! She kept looking round and round, searching for things where she had been accustomed to find them, and she looked as if something hurt her. I asked her if she didn't like it, and she said—

"'Oh, yes, it looks much more—more modern. Yes, dear, you have been very clever. It is quite—smart! A little bare, isn't it—just a little bare, don't you think?'

"'No, mother,' I said sternly, 'not the least little bit in the world! It seems so to you because you have had it so crowded that there was no room to move, but you will soon get accustomed to the room as it is, and like it far better.'

"'Yes, dear,' she said meekly, 'of—of course. I'm sure you are quite right,' and will you believe it, Una, she went straight into her own room, and cried! I know she did, for I saw the marks on her face later on, and taxed her with it. She was very apologetic, but she said the little table with the gold legs had been father's first gift to her after they were married, and she couldn't bear to have it put aside; and the ivory basket under the glass shade had come from the first French Exhibition, and she had worked those bead bannerettes herself when I was teething, and threatened with convulsions, and she did not dare to leave the house. Of course, I felt a wretch, and hugged her, and said—

"'Why didn't you say so before? We will bring them back at once, and put them where they were; but you have not tender associations with all the things. You did not work that hideous patchwork cushion, for instance, and—'

"'No, but Aunt Mary Ryley did,' she cried eagerly, 'and it is made out of pieces of all the dresses we wore when we were girls together. I often look at it and remember the happy times I had in the grey poplin and the puce silk.'

"So, of course, the cushion had to come back too, and by the end of a week every single thing was taken out of the cupboard, and put in its former place! They *all* had memories, and mother loved the memories, and cared nothing for the appearance. I was sweet about it. I wouldn't say so to anyone but you, Una, but I really was quite angelic, until one day when Amy Reeve came to call. She was staying with some friends a few miles off, and drove in to see me. You know how inquisitive Amy is, and how she stares, and takes in everything, and quizzes it afterwards? Well, my dear, she sat there, and her eyes simply roved round and round the whole time, until she must have known the furniture by heart. I suffered," sighed Lorna plaintively, "I suffered *anguish*! I wouldn't have minded anyone else so much—but Amy!"

I said, (properly), that Amy was a snob and an idiot, and that it mattered less than nothing what she thought, but all the time I knew that I should have felt humiliated myself, and Lorna knew it, too, but was not vexed with me for pretending the contrary, for it is only right to set a good example.

"Of course," she said, "one ought to be above such petty trials. If a friendship hangs upon chiffoniers and bead mats, it can't be worth keeping. I have told myself so ever since, but human nature is hard to kill, and I *should* have liked the house to look nice when Amy called! I despise myself for it, but I foresee that that room is going to be a continual trial. Its ugliness weighs upon me, and I feel self-conscious and uncomfortable every time my friends come to call, but I am not going to attempt any more changes. I wouldn't make the dear old mother cry again for fifty drawing-rooms!"

I thought it was sweet of her to talk like that, and wanted so badly to find a way out of the difficulty. I always feel there must be a way, and if one only thinks long enough it can generally be found. I sat plunged in thought, and at last the inspiration came.

"Didn't you say this room was your own to do with as you liked?"

"Yes; mother said I could have it for my den. Nobody uses it now; but, Una, it is hideous, too!"

"But it might be made pretty! It is small, and wouldn't take much furnishing. You could pick up a few odds and ends from other rooms that would not be missed."

"Oh, yes, mother wouldn't mind that, and the green felting on the floor is quite nice and new; but the paint, and the paper-saffron roses—and gold skriggles—and a light oak door! How could you possibly make anything look artistic against such a background?"

"You couldn't, and it wouldn't be much fun if you could. I've thought of something far more exciting. Lorna, let us paper and paint it ourselves! Let us go to town to-morrow, and choose the very, very most artistic and up-to-date paper that can be bought, and buy some tins of enamel, and turn workmen every morning. Oh, do! I should love it; and you were saying only an hour ago that you did not know how to amuse me in the mornings. If we did the room together you would always associate me with it, and I should feel as if it were partly mine, and be able to imagine just where you were sitting. Oh, do, Lorna! It would be such ripping sport!"

She didn't speak for a good half-minute, but just sat staring up in ecstasy of joy.

"You angel!" she cried at last. "You simple duck! How can you think of such lovely plans? Oh, Una, how have I lived without you all these months? Of course, I'll do it. I'd love to! I am never happier than when I am wrapped up in an apron with a brush in my hand.

I've enamelled things before now, but never hung a paper. Do you really think we could?"

"Of course! If the British workman can do it, there can't be much skill required, and we with our trained intelligence will soon overcome any difficulty," I said grandiloquently. "All we want is a pot of paste, and a pair of big scissors, and a table to lay the strips of paper on. I've seen it done scores of times."

"So have I," said Lorna. "And doesn't the paste smell! I expect, what with that and the enamel, we shall have no appetites left. It will spoil our complexions, too, very likely, and make us pale and sallow, but that doesn't matter."

I thought it mattered a good deal. It was all very well for her, but she wasn't staying with a friend who had an interesting grown-up brother. Even the finest natures can be inconsiderate sometimes.

Chapter Sixteen.

September 23rd.

The next morning we went to a paperhanger's shop and asked to see the very newest and most artistic designs in stock. There were lots of lovely things, but after great discussion we decided on a thick white paper, perfectly plain, except in each corner of the room, where there was a sort of conventional rose tree, growing up about seven feet high, with outstanding branches laden with the most exquisite pink roses. The white of the background was partly tinged with blue, with here and there a soft, irregular blue like a cloud. Looking up suddenly, you might imagine you were in the open air in the midst of a rose garden, and that would be a very pleasant delusion in Onslow Square.

The salesman asked how many pieces he should send, and whether we wished it hung at once. When I said we intended to hang it ourselves, he said—

"Oh, indeed, madam!" and looked unutterable things.

We were so quelled that we did not dare to ask him about the enamel and paste as we intended, but bought those at a modest little shop further on, and went home rejoicing.

Mrs Forbes had laughed and shaken all over in the most jovial manner when we told her of our plans, but she didn't approve of the white paper and paint, because, forsooth, it would get soiled. Of course it would get soiled! Things always do sooner or later. Old people are so dreadfully prudent that they get no pleasure out of life. When this paper is shabby Lorna can get a new one, or she may be married, or dead, or half a dozen different things. It's absurd to plan years ahead. I cheered up poor Lorna, who is of a sensitive nature and easily depressed, and when she recovered asked what she thought we ought to do next.

"The first thing to settle," she said decidedly, "is Midas! He can help us in a dozen ways if he will, for he is really wonderfully handy for a boy of his age. He will do nothing unless we consult him formally, and make a definite business arrangement, but it pleases him and won't hurt us, as it will be only a few coppers. He is saving up for a motor-car at the present moment, and Wallace says that by steady attention to business he really believes he will get one by the time he is sixty."

We called Midas in and consulted him professionally. He is tall and lanky, and has pale blue eyes with long light eyelashes. You would think to look at him that he was a gentle, unworldly creature, addicted to poetry, but he isn't! He sat astride the table and viewed the landscape o'er.

"The first thing will be to take every stick of furniture out of the room, and have the carpet up. I know what girls are when they do jobs of this kind. You will be up to your eyes in paste, and it won't be safe to leave anything within touching distance. The furniture must be removed and stored. I'll store it for you in my room. Then you'll need a ladder, and some planks for the lengths of paper to lie on while you paste 'em. I'll hire you the old shutter from the drawing-room."

"The shutters are as much mine as yours," said Lorna. "I don't need to hire them; I can have them if I want!"

"That's where you show your ignorance, my dear. They are in my possession, and I won't give them up without compensation. Then you'll need a man to assist in the hanging!"

"Say a boy at once, and name your price, and be done with it. You are a regular Shylock!"

Midas grinned as if pleased with the compliment, drew a pocket-book and a stubby end of a pencil from his pocket, and began alternately stroking his chin and jotting down words and figures. Lorna grimaced at me behind his back, but kept a stern expression for his benefit. I suppose she knew that if he saw her smile prices would go up. Presently he drew a line, tore the leaf out of the book and handed it across with a bow.

"My estimate, ladies! It is always more satisfactory to have an agreement beforehand."

I peeped over Lorna's shoulder and read—

Estimate For Proposed Renovations.

To Removal of furniture	1	9
Storage of same at rate of 6 pence per day	1	6
Restoration of same	1	9
Impliments	1	0
Man's time	1	3
Sundrys		6
	7	9

It was quite a formidable total, but Lorna was evidently accustomed to extortionate demands, and began beating him down without delay.

"Well, of all the outrageous pieces of impudence! Seven and ninepence, indeed! You must have taken leave of your senses. If you think I am going to pay you four or five shillings for carrying a few odds and ends of furniture along the passage, you are mightily mistaken! And we should have to help you, too, for you couldn't manage alone. If we asked Wallace he'd do it at once, without any pay at all."

"Drink to me only with thine eyes!" chanted the little wretch, folding his arms and gazing fixedly at me with a life-like assumption of Wallace's attitude and expression, which sent Lorna into fits of laughter, and made me magenta with embarrassment. "If you like to wait until Wallace has time to run your errands and see you through your difficulties, you will get your room finished by Christmas — with luck! I am sorry you think my charges high, but I'm afraid I don't see my way to reduce 'em."

"Midas, don't be a goose! We will pay you twopence an hour for your time, and twopence a day for storage — that's the limit. That disposes of the first four items. As for the rest, we had better understand each other before we go any further. Kindly distinguish between implements and sundries."

"Is this an Oxford local, or is it a conversation between a brother and sister?" Midas demanded, throwing back his head, and mutely appealing to an unseen arbiter in the corner of the ceiling. "If you can't understand a simple thing like that, it doesn't say much for your education. It is easily seen *you* were never a plumber! I thought we were going to come to a friendly agreement, but you are so close and grasping, there is no dealing with you. Look here, will you give me half-a-crown for the job?"

I gasped with surprise at this sudden and sweeping reduction of terms, but Lorna said calmly —

"Done! A halfpenny discount if paid within the hour!" and they shook hands with mutual satisfaction.

"Cheap at the price!" was Lorna's comment, as the contractor left the room, and before the next few days were over I heartily agreed with this opinion. Midas was an ideal workman, grudging neither time nor pains to accomplish his task in a satisfactory manner. His long arms and strong wrists made light of what would have been heavy tasks for us, and the dirtier he grew the more he enjoyed it. It must be dreadful to live in a town! Lorna assured me plaintively that the room had been thoroughly spring-cleaned at Easter, but I should have thought it had happened nearer the Flood. I swallowed pecks of dust, and my hands grew raw with washing before we began to paint. I thought we should never have finished enamelling that room. The first coat made hardly any impression on the background, and we had to go over it again and again before we got anything like a good effect. To a casual observer it looked really very nice, but we knew where to look for shortcomings, and I grew hot whenever anyone looked at a certain panel in the door.

Then we set to work on the paper. First you cut it into lengths. It seems quite easy, but it isn't, because you waste yards making the patterns meet, and then you haven't enough, and you go into town to buy more, and they haven't it in stock, and it has to be ordered, and you sit and champ, and can't get any further.

Then you make the paste. It smells horrid, and do what you will, cover yourself as best you can, it gets up to the eyes! We wore two old holland skirts of Lorna's, quite short and trig, and washing shirts, and huge print wrappers; but before we had been working for an hour our fingers were glued together; then we yawned or sneezed and put our hands to our faces, and *they* were stickied. Then bits of hair—"tendrils" as they call them in books—fell down, and we fastened them up, and our hair got as bad. We were spectacles!

A kettle was kept on the hob, and we were continually bathing our hands in hot water, for, of course, we dared not touch the outside of the paper unless they were quite clean, and the table wanted washing before each fresh strip was laid down, as the paste had always oozed off the edges of the last piece. There is one thing sure and certain: I shall never take up paper-hanging as a profession.

The hanging itself is really rather exciting. Midas climbed to the top of the ladder and held the top of the strip in position; Lorna crouched beneath, and guided it in the way it should go, so as to meet the edge of the one before, and I stood on a chair and smoothed it down and down with a clean white cloth. Doing it with great care like this, we got no wrinkles at all, and when the first side of the room was finished, it looked so professional that we danced—literally danced—for joy.

By the end of the afternoon it was done, and so were we! Simply so tired we could hardly stand, but mentally we were full of triumph, for that room was a picture to behold. We ran out into the passage and brought in everyone we could find, servants and charwoman included. Then they made remarks, and we stood and listened.

The cook said, "My, Miss Lorna, wouldn't the pattern go round?" The charwoman said, "I like a bit of gilding meself. It looks 'andsome." The parlourmaid said, "How will the furniture look against it, miss?" which was really the nastiest hit of all; only the little Tweeny stared and flushed, and rolled her hands in her apron, and said, "All them roses on the wall! It would be like a Bank-'oliday to sit aside 'em!"

Tweeny has the soul of a poet. I bought her some flowers the very next time I went out. Wallace came in and twiddled his moustache, and said—

"By Jove, is it really done! Aren't you dead beat? I say, Miss Sackville, don't do any more to-day. It's too bad of Lorna to work you like this. I shall interfere in my professional capacity."

He was far too much engrossed in Una Sackville to have any eyes for the paper.

Mrs Forbes thought, like the cook, that it was a pity that the pattern didn't go round; and the dear old doctor tip-toed up and down, jingled the money in his pockets, and said—

"Eh, what? Eh, what? Something quite novel, eh! Didn't go in for things of this sort in my young days. Very smart indeed, my dear, very smart! Now I suppose you will be wanting some new fixings," (his hand came slowly out of his waistcoat pocket, and my hopes ran mountains high). "Mustn't spoil the ship for a penn'orth of tar, you know. There, that will help to buy a few odds and ends."

He put something into Lorna's hand; she looked at it, flushed red with delight, and hugged him rapturously round the neck. After he had gone she showed it to me with an air of triumph, and it was—half-a-sovereign! I expected several pounds, and had hard work not to show my disappointment, but I suppose ten shillings means as much to Lorna as ten pounds to me. Well, I am not at all sure that you don't get more fun out of planning and contriving to make a little money go a long way, than in simply going to a shop and ordering what you want. Lorna's worldly wealth amounted, with the half-sovereign, to seventeen and six-pence, and with this lordly sum for capital we set to work to transform the room.

Chapter Seventeen.

I have told all our experiences in papering the room together, because they seemed to come better that way; but, of course, lots of other things have been happening at the same time. One evening we went to a concert, and another time some friends came in after dinner, and we played games and had music. I sang a great deal, and everyone seemed to like listening, and my dress was the prettiest in the room, and all the men wanted to talk to me, and it was most agreeable.

On Sunday we went to an ugly town church, but the vicar had a fine, good face, and I liked his sermon. He seemed to believe in you, and expect you to do great things, and that is always inspiring. Some clergymen keep telling you how bad you are, and personally that puts my back up, and I begin to think I am not half so black as I am painted; but when this dear man took for granted that you were unselfish and diligent, and deeply in earnest about good things, I felt first ashamed, and then eager to try again, and fight the sins that do so terribly easily beset me. I sang the last hymn in a sort of fervour, and came out into the cool night air positively longing for a battle in which I could win my spurs, and oh dear, dear, in ten minutes' time, before we were half-way home, I was flirting with Wallace, and talking of frivolous worldly subjects, as if I had never had a serious thought in my life!

It's so terribly hard to remember, and keep on remembering when one is young, but God must surely understand. I don't think He will be angry. He knows that deep, deep down I want most of all to be good!

Wallace is nice and kind and clever, and I like him to like me, but I could never by any possibility like him—seriously, I mean! I can't tell why; it's just one of the mysterious things that comes by instinct when you grow up to be a woman. There is a great gulf thousands of miles wide between the man you just like and the man you could love; but sometimes the man you could love doesn't want you, and it is wrong even to think of him, and then it's a temptation to be extra nice to the other one, because his devotion soothes your wounded feelings.

I suppose Miss Bruce would call it love of admiration, and wish me to snub the poor fellow, and keep him at arm's length, but I don't see why I should. It would be conceited to take for granted that he was seriously in love, and I don't see why I shouldn't enjoy myself when I get a chance. It's only fun, of course, but I do enjoy playing off little experiments upon Wallace, to test my power over him, and then to watch the result! For example, at lunch-time I express a casual wish for a certain thing, and before four o'clock it is in my possession; or I show an interest in an entertainment, and tickets appear as if by magic. It is quite exciting. I feel as if I were playing a thrilling new game.

The room is almost furnished, and it looks sweet. One can hardly believe it is the same dreary little den that I saw on that first evening. We stole, (by kind permission), one or two chairs, a writing-table, and a dear little Indian cabinet from the overcrowded drawing-room, and with some help from Midas manufactured the most scrumptious cosy-corner out of old packing-cases and cushions covered with rose-coloured brocade. We put a deep frill of the same material, mounted on a thin brass rail, on the wall above the mantelpiece, and arranged Lorna's best ornaments and nick-nacks against this becoming background. It did not seem quite appropriate to the garden idea to hang pictures on the walls, which is just as well, as she hasn't got any, but I bought her a tall green pedestal and flower-pot and a big branching palm as my contribution to the room, and as she says, "It gives the final touch of luxury to the whole." I could wish for a new fender and fire-irons, and a few decent rugs, but you can't have everything in this wicked world, and really, at night when the lamp-light sends a rosy glow through the newly-covered shade, (only muslin, but it looks like silk!) you could not wish to see a prettier room.

Lorna is awfully sweet about it. She said to me, "It was your idea, Una. I shall always feel that it was your gift, and every pleasant hour

I spend here will be another link in the chain which binds us together. This visit of yours will be memorable, in more ways than one!" and she looked at me in a meaning fashion which I hated. How more ways than one, pray? I hope to goodness she is not getting any foolish notions in her head. She might know me better by this time.

I don't know why it is, but I am always depressed after a letter from home. Mother reports that there is no improvement in Vere's health, and that her spirits are variable—sometimes low, sometimes quite bright and hopeful. Mr Dudley is very good in coming to see her, and his visits always cheer her up. He asked after me last time, hoped that I was enjoying myself and would not hurry back. I am not wanted there apparently, and here they all love having me, and implore me to stay on. I wasn't sure if I wanted to, but I've decided that I will since that last letter arrived. I told Mrs Forbes this morning that I would stay a fortnight longer, and she kissed me and looked quite unreasonably relieved. I can't see how it matters much to her!

Such a curious thing happened that night, when Wallace and I were talking about books, and discussing the heroine in a novel which he had given me to read.

"Did she remind you of anyone?" he asked, and when I said "No," "Why, she is you to the life! Appearance, manner, character—everything. It might have been meant for a portrait," he declared. "I was reading it over last night, and the likeness is extraordinary."

I privately determined to read the book over again on the first opportunity to discover what I seemed like to other people. The heroine is supposed to be very pretty and charming, but personally I had thought her rather silly, so I did not know whether to feel complimented or not. I determined to introduce the subject to Lorna, and see if she could throw any light upon it, and she did! More light than I appreciated!

"Oh, I liked Nan very well," she said, "but not nearly so much as Wallace did. He simply raved about her and declared that if he ever met a girl like that in real life he should fall desperately in love with her on the spot. She is his ideal of everything that a girl should be."

"Oh!" I said blankly. For a moment I felt inclined to tell Lorna everything, but something stopped me, and I am thankful that it did. It would be so horrid to feel she was watching all the time. For once in my life I was glad when she went away, and I was left alone to think.

"Desperately in love!" Can Wallace really be that, and with me? It makes me go hot and cold just to think of it, and my heart thumps with agitation. I don't feel happy exactly, but very excited and important. I have such a lonely feeling sometimes, and I do so long for someone to love me best of all. At home, though they are all kind enough, I am always second fiddle, if not third, and it is nice to be appreciated! I could never care for Wallace in that way, but I like him to like me. It makes things interesting, and I was feeling very flat and dejected, and in need of something to cheer me up. Of course, I don't want to do anything wrong, but Wallace is so young, only twenty-four, and has no money, so he couldn't think of being married or anything silly like that; besides, I've heard it is good for boys to have a fancy for a nice girl—it keeps them steady.

In any case, I have promised to stay on for another fortnight, and I couldn't alter my mind and go away now without making a fuss, and if I stay I can't be disagreeable, so I must just behave as if Lorna had never repeated that stupid remark. I dare say, if the truth were known, Wallace has fancied himself in love with half-a-dozen girls before now, and it would be ridiculous of me to imagine anything serious. Anyway, I don't care. I have thought of nothing but other people for months back, and they don't seem to miss me a bit, but only hope I won't hurry back. I'm tired of it. Now I am going to enjoy myself, and I don't care what happens!

Chapter Eighteen.

It is ten days since I wrote anything in this diary, and to-night, when I opened it in my misery, hoping to find some comfort in writing down my thoughts, the first thing that met my eyes were those dreadful words, "I am going to enjoy myself, and I don't care what happens." Enjoy myself, indeed! I have never been so miserable in my life. I never knew before what misery meant, even on that awful night of the fire, when we didn't know whether Vere would live or die. Troubles with which one has nothing to do, which come, as it were, straight from God, can never make one feel like this. There is no remorse in them, and no guilt, and no burning, intolerable shame.

What would Miss Bruce think of her pupil now? What would father think? What would Rachel—"the best woman in the world"—think of me to-night?

I am going to make myself write it all down, and then, if I ever try to gloss it over to myself or others in the future, this written account will be here to give me the lie. Here it is, then, bold and plain—

"I have broken a man's heart for the sake of a little fun and excitement for myself, and as a sop to my wounded vanity!"

It makes me shiver to read the words, for I did not realise the full meanness of what I was doing until the end came, and I woke with a shock to see myself as I really am. All these last ten days I have been acting a part to myself as well as to others, pretending to be unconscious of danger, but I knew—oh, I knew perfectly well! I think a girl must always know when a man loves her. I knew it by the tone of Wallace's voice, by the light in his eyes, by the change which came over his looks and manner the moment I appeared. It was like a game, a horrible new game which fascinated me against my will, and I could not bear to end it. Every night when I said my prayers I determined to turn over a new leaf next day, but when the next day came I put on my prettiest clothes and did my hair the way he liked it best, and sang his favourite songs, and was all smiles and sweetness. Oh, what a Pharisee I am! In this very book I have denounced Vere for her flirtations and greed of admiration, and then I have succumbed to the very first temptation, without so much as a struggle. I shall never, never be able to hold up my head again. I feel too contemptible to live.

Last night things came to a crisis. Wallace and Lorna and I went to a party given by some intimate family friends. Wallace had asked me in the morning what colour I was going to wear, and just before dinner he came into the drawing-room and presented me with a spray of the most lovely pink roses. I think he expected to find me alone, but the whole family was assembled, and it was most embarrassing to see how seriously they took it. At home we have loads of flowers in the conservatories, but sometimes one of Vere's admirers sends her a lot of early violets, or lilies of the valley, great huge boxes which must cost a small fortune, but no one thinks anything of it, or pays any attention beyond a casual remark. Here, however, it was different.

"Roses!" ejaculated Lorna, in a tone of awe-stricken astonishment.

Midas whistled softly, and Mrs Forbes looked first at Wallace and then at me—in a wistful, anxious kind of way, which made me feel inclined to run home on the spot. I determined to make some excuse and depart suddenly some day soon, while Wallace was out on his rounds, but it was too late. I was not allowed to escape so easily as that.

During the evening Wallace took me into the conservatory to see the flowers, and it was not my fault that everyone went out and left us alone. I tried to be cold and chilling, but that only made him anxious to discover what was wrong.

"It is my fault! I know quite well it is my fault," he cried, bending over me, his face so drawn and puckered with anxiety that he looked quite old. "I am a stupid, blundering fellow, and you have been an angel to be so sweet and forbearing. I am not fit to come near you, but I would rather cut off my right hand than hurt you in any way. You know that, don't you, Una?"

He had never called me Una before, and he looked so different from the calm, complacent youth I had known a few weeks before—so much older and more formidable, that it was difficult to believe it could be the same person. I was frightened, but tried hard to appear cool and self-possessed.

"I am not vexed at all. On the contrary, I am enjoying myself very much. The flowers are lovely. I always—"

It was no use. He seized my hand, and cried pleadingly—

"Don't put me off, Una; don't trifle with me. It's too serious for that. You are cold to me to-night, and it has come to this, that I cannot live when you are not kind. What has changed you since this afternoon? Were you vexed with me for bringing you those roses?"

"Not in the least, so far as I am concerned; but your people seemed astonished. It made me feel a little awkward."

He looked at once relieved and puzzled. "But they know!" he cried. "They know quite well. They would not be astonished at my giving you anything. Has Lorna never told you that she knows?"

"I really fail to understand what there is to know," I said, sitting up very straight and stiff, looking as haughty and unapproachable as I possibly could. It was coming very close. I knew it, though I never had the experience before, and I would have given anything in the world to escape. Oh, how can girls like to have proposals from men whom they don't mean to accept? How can they bring themselves to boast of them as if they were a triumph and a pride? I never felt so humiliated in my life as I did when I sat there and listened to Wallace's wild words.

"What is there to know? Only that I love you with all my heart and strength—that I have loved you ever since the moment I first saw your sweet face. You did not seem like a stranger, for I had been waiting for you all my life. Oh, Una, these few weeks have been like a dream of happiness. I never knew what it was to live before. You are so—"

I haven't the heart to repeat all the praises the poor fellow lavished upon me while I sat listening in an agony of shame, feeling more and more miserable every moment, as I realised that, in spite of his agitation, he was by no means despondent as to the result of his wooing. He seemed more anxious to assure me of his devotion than to question me about mine, as if he imagined that my coldness was caused by pique or jealousy. I drew away my hands, and tried to stop him by vague murmurs of dissent, but it was no use, he only became more eager and determined.

"We all love you, Una. My mother thinks you the most charming girl she has ever met. She was speaking of you to me only last night; she feels naturally a little sad, poor mother! to know that she is no longer the first consideration to her boy, but she quite understands. And the pater, too—he is in love with you himself. Who could help it, darling?"

"Oh, stop, stop! I can't bear it. You must not talk like that," I cried desperately. "You are taking everything for granted, and it is impossible, quite impossible. I don't want to marry anyone. I'm too young. I must wait for years before I can even think of such a thing."

He looked actually relieved, instead of disappointed, as my words evidently removed one big difficulty from his path.

"I couldn't ask you to marry me yet, dearest. I have my way to make, and could not provide a home that would be worthy of you for some years to come; but as you say, we are both young, and can afford to wait; and oh, Una, I could work like ten men with such a prospect to inspire me. I will get on for your sake; it is in me, I know it is—I shall succeed!"

"I hope you may, I'm sure," I said, nearly crying with agitation and misery. "But you must not think of me. I have nothing to do with it. I like you very much, but I couldn't marry you now or ever—I never thought of such a thing—it's quite impossible. You must, please, please, never speak of it again!"

Even then he wouldn't understand, but preferred to think that I was shy, nervous, coy—anything rather than simply and absolutely truthful. He began again in a humble, pleading voice, which tore my heart.

"I know it seems presumption to ask so much. I am an insignificant nobody, and you might marry anyone you liked. In every sense of the word but one I am a wretched match for you, but love counts for something, and you will never find anyone to love you more. I'd give my very life to serve you, and I will give it, if you will trust yourself to me! My father was no older than I am when he became engaged, and he told me only the other day that he looked back on that hour as the beginning of his success. He would be glad to see me engaged also."

"Have you spoken about me to him, then, as well as to your mother?" I demanded testily. I felt so guilty about my own conduct that it was a relief to be able to find fault with someone else, and I worked myself up into quite a show of indignation. "You must have made very sure of my answer to be ready to discuss me in such a general fashion. It would have been more courteous to wait until you had my permission. You have placed us both in a most awkward position, for, as I said before, I could never marry you. It is quite impossible. I like you very much, but not in that way. Let us be friends, and forget everything else. We were so happy as we were— it is such a pity to spoil it all like this."

"Spoil it!" he repeated blankly. He had grown quite white while I was speaking, and his eyes had a dazed, startled expression. "Does it spoil things for you, Una, to know that I love you? But you have known that for a long time—everyone in the house found it out, and you could not have helped seeing it, too. You say I have made too sure of you. Forgive me, darling, but if I have done so it is only because I know you are too sweet and good to encourage a man when there was no hope. I am more sorry than I can say if I have annoyed you by speaking to my parents, but the mater naturally spoke to me when she saw how things were going, and I had to consult my father about ways and means. Una, darling, you don't mean it. You can't mean to break my heart after leading me on all these weeks?"

"I never led you on!" I cried vainly. "I was only nice to you as I would have been to anyone else. I knew you liked me; but everyone who is kind and attentive does not want to marry one as a matter of course. It would be horrid to expect it. Lorna is my friend, and you are her brother, so of course—"

He looked me full in the face and said slowly—

"It will be difficult to believe—but if you will tell me just once quite simply and plainly, I will take your word, Una. Don't protest, please—tell me truthfully, once for all: did you, or did you not, know I loved you with all my heart?"

I wanted to say "No." In a sense I could have said it truthfully enough, for I had no definite knowledge, but I remembered what Lorna had told me about the heroine in the novel; I remembered Mrs Forbes's wistful manner, and oh, a dozen little incidents too small to be written down, when Wallace's own manner had told the truth only too plainly. He was staring at me, poor boy, with his wan, miserable eyes, and I could not tell a lie. I began to cry in a feeble, helpless kind of way, and faltered out, "I—I thought you did, but I couldn't be sure. You know I couldn't be sure, and it was only for a little while! I am going home so soon that I didn't think it could matter."

He leant forward, leaning his head on his hands.

"Shall I tell you how much it matters?" he asked huskily. "It matters just this, that you have spoilt my life! There was not a happier, more contented fellow living than I was—before you came. I loved my work, and loved my home. I intended to succeed in my profession, and the future was full of interest. I would not have changed places with any man on earth. Now!" he held out his right hand and snapped his fingers expressively, "it is over; the zest is out of it all if you are not there. If I had met you anywhere else it might have been easier, but you have come right into the middle of my life, and if I would I shall not be able to forget you. Every morning when I come down to breakfast I shall look across the table and imagine you sitting facing me; I shall see you wherever I go—like a ghost—in every room in the house, in everything I do. That is the price I have to pay for your amusement. You have made a fool of me, you whom I thought the type of everything that was true and womanly. You knew that I loved you, but it didn't matter to you what I suffered. You were going home soon—you would not see it. It didn't matter!"

"No, no, no!" I cried in agony. "It isn't true. I am bad enough, but not a heartless monster. I will tell you the whole truth. I was miserable myself when I came here; ill and tired out, and sore because—because they didn't care for me at home as much as I wanted. I always want people to like me. I did at school—Lorna will tell you that I did; and when you were nice to me it cheered me up, and made me happy again. I never dreamt that it was serious until a little time ago—last week—and even then I did not think you could possibly want to marry me—you were too young—you had no home—"

"No, that is true. I am no match for Miss Sackville. I was a fool to forget it. Thank you for reminding me," he interrupted bitterly.

Poor boy—oh, poor boy, he looked so miserable—it made me ache to see his white, changed face. He looked so handsome, too; so much more of a man than he had ever done before. I looked at him and wondered why it was that I could not care for him as he wished. Had I been too hasty in deciding that it was impossible? He wanted me, and no one else did; and it would be nice to be engaged and have someone to love me best of all. Perhaps I should grow to love him too; I always do like people who like me; and Lorna would be so pleased. She would be my real sister, and could come and stay with me in my own home. I was so upset and miserable, so stung by Wallace's taunt about his poverty, that I was just in the mind to be reckless. His hand lay limply by his side, and in a sudden gush of tenderness and pity I slid my arm beneath it and said softly, "Don't be cross with me! I never thought for one moment if you were poor or rich. That doesn't matter a bit. If I have made you miserable, I am miserable too. If you want me to be engaged to you—I will, and I'll try to like you. Please, please do not look like that! If I promise it will be all right, and you will forgive me for being so thoughtless, won't you, Wallace?"

He turned his head and stared at me steadily. The anger died out of his face, but he looked dreadfully sad.

"Poor Una," he said, "how little you understand! Do you think I am such a cad as to accept such an offer as that? I love you and want you to be happy, not miserable as you would certainly be if you were engaged to a man you had to 'try to like.' Thank you for the offer all the same. It will comfort me a little to remember that at any rate you felt kindly towards me. It is no use saying any more. My dream is over, and I shall have to bear the awakening as well as I can. A fellow cannot expect to have everything his own way. I don't want to whine. Shall we go back to the house?"

"In a minute—one minute—only tell me first that you forgive me, and if there is nothing at all that I can do to help you, and show how wretchedly, wretchedly sorry I am!"

"Forgive you?" he repeated sadly. "I love you, Una. I can forgive you, I expect, a good deal more easily than you will forgive yourself. Yes, there is something you can do—if you ever discover that another poor fellow is in love with you—and you are the sort of girl whom men will love—remember me and spare him this experience. Don't go on being 'nice' to him. That kind of niceness is the worst form of cruelty."

I hung my head and could not answer. To think that "that boy," as I had contemptuously called him, should have behaved in such a manly, generous fashion! I felt utterly ashamed and despicable. It was he who is a thousand times too good for me!

Chapter Nineteen.

We were very silent driving home in the brougham, and I refused to go into Lorna's room, as I always did before going to bed, saying that I was too tired to talk. She looked anxious, but did not try to persuade me. I afterwards learnt that she went to Wallace instead, and sat up with him for the greater part of the night.

I lay wide awake tossing and crying until five o'clock, when I fell asleep, and did not wake until nine. Lorna did not come to see me, and, though I dreaded her coming, I felt miserable because she stayed away. Every single morning she had come into my room and hugged and kissed me, and we had walked down to breakfast arm-in-arm. She must have been very, very angry to omit that ceremony!

I took a long time to dress, for I wanted Wallace to be safely started on his rounds before appearing downstairs, and at last, just as I was feeling that I could not respectably linger another moment, the door opened, and there, at last, stood Lorna.

She had been crying dreadfully. I could see that at a glance, for the eyelids were swollen and puffy, just as they used to be the first morning after our return to school. Mine were swollen, too, and we stood staring miserably at each other, but not approaching a step nearer, until at last she said coldly—

"Mother sent me upstairs to ask if you would prefer to have your breakfast in bed. She thought you were not up."

"Oh, yes, I have been waiting. Lorna, don't look at me like that!" I cried desperately. "I'm miserable too, and you ought not to turn against me—you are my friend."

"Wallace is my brother," said Lorna simply. Her lip quivered. "I sat up with him until four o'clock this morning. He has always been such a happy, cheerful boy. I did not know he could be so miserable.

If you could have seen and heard him talk, you would have felt broken-hearted for him—even you!"

"Even you!" I repeated reproachfully. "Am I a monster, Lorna, that you talk to me like that? Can't you understand that I feel a hundred times worse than you can possibly do? I never, never thought that when I was in trouble you would be the first person to turn against me."

"Neither did I. I have been too fond of you, Una. I admired you so much, and was so proud of having you for my friend that I have been unjust to other people for your sake. I often took your part at school when I knew you were in the wrong, simply because I was afraid of making you angry. It was cowardly of me, and this is my reward! Oh, Una, you say you are sorry, but you knew it was coming! You are too clever not to have seen it long ago. If it had been another man I should have spoken out, but a brother is almost like oneself, so one can't interfere. But I hinted—you know I hinted, Una—and I saw by your face that you understood. If you didn't care for him, why didn't you go home when it was first arranged? We all took it as a good sign when you agreed to stay on, and Wallace was so happy about it. Poor boy! He will never be happy again. He says he will go abroad, and father has been looking forward all these years to his help. It will break his heart if he loses Wallace!"

Everyone was broken-hearted, it seemed, and they all blamed me, and said it was my fault. I felt inclined to jump out of the window, and put an end to it at once. I did turn towards it, and I must have looked pretty desperate, for Lorna came forward quickly, and took hold of me by the arm.

"Come down and talk to mother. She is all alone, and she is old and will understand better than I do. Oh, Una, I shall always love you! I shan't be able to help it, whatever you have done. I didn't mean to be unkind, but I am—so—miserable!"

I gripped her hand, but couldn't speak; we were both struggling not to cry all the way downstairs, and I couldn't eat any breakfast; I felt as if I could never eat again. Mrs Forbes came into the room just as I left the table, and Lorna went out at once, as if by a previous arrangement. It was awful! Mrs Forbes looked so old and ill and worried, and she was so kind. I could have borne it better if she had been cross to me.

"Sit down, dear. Come close to the fire, your hands feel cold," she said, pushing me gently into an easy chair, and poking the coals into a blaze. "You and I want a little talk to each other, I think, and we shall be quite uninterrupted here. My poor boy has told me of his disappointment, but, indeed, he did not need to tell me. I could see what had happened by his face. I am very disappointed, too. I thought he would have very different news to tell me, and I should have been very happy to welcome you as a daughter. We have known you by name for so many years that you did not seem like a stranger even when you first arrived, and we have been very happy together these five weeks—"

"Oh, very happy! I have had a lovely time. I shall never forget how happy I have been."

She looked at me anxiously, her eyebrows knitted together.

"Then if you have been so happy, I do not see why— Let us speak out, dear, and understand each other thoroughly. My boy and I have always been close friends, and if I am to be of help or comfort to him now I must understand how this trouble has come about. Wallace is not conceited—he has a very modest estimation of his own merits, but he seems to have expected a different answer. Sometimes in these affairs young people misunderstand each other, and little sorenesses arise, which a few outspoken words can smooth away. If I could act as peacemaker between you two, I should be very thankful. My children's happiness is my first consideration nowadays. If there is anything I can do, just tell me honestly. Speak out as you would to your own mother."

But I had nothing to tell. I shook my head, and faltered nervously—

"No, there is nothing—we have had no quarrels. I like Wallace very much, oh, very much indeed, but not—I could never—I couldn't be anything more than his friend."

"Is there then someone else whom you care for?"

There were several people, but I couldn't exactly say so to her—it seemed so rude. Wallace was a nice, kind boy, but he couldn't compare for interest with—Jim Carstairs, for instance, dear, silent, loyal, patient Jim, who gives all, and asks nothing in return, or even jolly little Mr Nash, who is always happy and smiling, and trying to make other people happy. I like them both better than Wallace, to say nothing of— And then a picture rose before me of a tall, lean figure dressed in a tweed shooting-suit, of a sunburnt face, out of which looked blue eyes, which at one moment would twinkle with laughter, and at the next grow stern and grave and cold. They could soften, too, and look wonderfully tender. I had seen them like that just once or twice when he looked at me, and said, "Una!" and at the remembrance, for some stupid reason the blood rushed to my face, and there I sat blushing, blushing, blushing, until my very ears tingled with heat.

I said nothing, and Mrs Forbes said nothing, but looking up at the end of a horrid silence, I saw that her face had entirely changed in expression since I had seen it last. All the softness had left it; she looked the image of wounded dignity.

"I understand! There is nothing more to say, then, except that if you were so very sure of your own feelings, I cannot understand how it is that you have allowed the matter to get this length. I am thankful to know that my boy's principles are strong enough to prevent his disappointment doing him any real harm. It might have been very different with many young men. At the best it is a hard thing for us to see his young life clouded, and you will understand that it is our duty to protect him from further suffering. You will not think me inhospitable if I suggest that your visit had better come to an end at once."

My cheeks burnt. It was humiliation indeed to be told to go in that summary fashion, but I knew I deserved it, and I should have been thankful to leave that very moment.

"I will go to-day. There is a train at one o'clock. I can send a telegram from the station, and tell mother I am coming. I will go up-stairs now and pack," I cried, and she never protested a bit, but said quite quietly that she would order a cab to take me to the station. Talk about feeling small! I simply cringed as I went out of that room.

The carriage was waiting for me at the station at the end of a miserable journey, but no one was in it. I had hoped that father would come to meet me. I could have spoken to him, and he would have understood. John said he was out for the day with a shooting-party, and when I reached the house another disappointment awaited me, for I was met by an announcement that mother also had been obliged to go out to keep an engagement.

"She hopes to be home by five o'clock," said the servant. "Miss Vere and Lady Mary are in the blue sitting-room. Mr Dudley has just come to call."

I had forgotten that Lady Mary was staying at the house, and it made me feel as if I were more superfluous than ever, for Vere would not need me when she had her best friend at hand, and, somehow or other, Will Dudley was just the last person in the world I wanted to see just then. There was nothing for it, however; I had to go upstairs and stand the horrible ordeal of being cross-questioned about my unexpected return.

"Don't tell me it is an outbreak of small-pox!" cried Lady Mary, huddling back in her chair, and pretending to shudder at my approach. "That's the worst of staying in a doctor's house—you simply court infection! If it's anything interesting and becoming, you may kiss me as usual, but if it's small-pox or mumps, I implore you to keep at the other end of the room! I'm not sure that mumps wouldn't be the worse of the two. I can't endure to look fat!"

"Has Lorna turned out a villain in disguise? Have you quarrelled and bidden each other a tragic farewell?" asked Vere laughingly.

She looked thinner than ever, but her cheeks were flushed, and her eyes as bright as stars. As for Will Dudley, he stared at the pattern of the carpet, and his eyebrows twitched in the impatient way I know so well. I think he saw that I was really in trouble, and was vexed with the girls for teasing me.

"Thank you, everyone was quite well when I left. You need not be afraid of infection, and Lorna is nicer than ever. We have certainly not quarrelled."

"Then why this thusness?" asked Lady Mary, and Vere burst into a laugh.

"Scalps, Babs, scalps! I see it all! My mind misgave me as soon as I heard of the fascinating Wallace. And was it really so serious that you had to fly at a moment's notice?"

I simply got up and marched out of the room. It was too much to bear. I sat in my own room all alone for over an hour, and hated everybody. Oh, I *was* miserable!

---

11 PM.

I have been thinking seriously over things, and have decided to put away this diary, and not write in it any more for six months or a year. It will be better so, for at present I am in such a wretched, unsettled state of mind that what I write would not be edifying, but only painful to read in time to come.

I've been reading over the first few pages to-night, and they seem written by quite a different person—a happy, self-confident, complacent Una, who felt perfectly satisfied of coming triumphantly through any and every situation. This Una is a very crestfallen, humble-minded creature, who knows she has failed, and dreads failing again; but I want to be good, through it all I long to be good! O dear God, who loves me, and understands, take pity on me, and show me the way!

Chapter Twenty.

June 15th.

To-day the first roses have opened in the garden, the rose-garden at the Moat; for we came home two months ago, and are still luxuriating in the old haunts and the new rooms, which are as beautiful as money and mother's beautiful taste can make them. I felt a sort of rush of happiness as I buried my face in the cool, fragrant leaves, and, somehow or other, a longing came over me to unearth this old diary, and write the history of the year.

It has been a long, long winter. We spent three months in Bournemouth for Vere's sake, taking her to London to see the specialist on our way home. He examined her carefully, and said that spinal troubles were slow affairs, that it was a great thing to keep up the general health, that he was glad we had been to Bournemouth, and that no doubt the change home would also be beneficial. Fresh air, fresh air—live as much in the fresh open air as possible during the summer— Then he stopped, and Vere looked at him steadily, and said—

"You mean that I am worse?"

"My dear young lady, you must not be despondent. Hope on, hope ever! You can do more for yourself than any doctor. These things take time. One never knows when the turn may come," he said, reeling off the old phrases which we all knew so well—oh, so drearily well—by this time.

Vere closed her eyes and turned her head aside with the saddest, most pitiful little smile. She has been very good on the whole, poor dear, during the winter—less cynical and hard in manner, though she still refuses to speak of her illness, and shrinks with horror from anything like pity.

The night after that doctor's visit I heard a muffled sound from her room next door to mine, and crept in to see what was wrong. She was sobbing to herself, great, gasping, heart-broken sobs, the sound of which haunt me to this day, and when I put my arms round her, instead of shaking me off, she clung to me with the energy of despair.

"What is it, darling?" I asked, and she panted out broken sentences.

"The doctor! I have been longing to see him; I thought I was better, that he would be pleased with my progress, but it's no use—I can see it is no use! He has no hope. I shall be like this all my life. Babs, *think* of it! I am twenty-three, and I may live until I am seventy—upon this couch! Oh, I shall go mad—I am going mad—I can't bear it a moment longer. The last ten months have seemed like a life-time, but if it goes on year after year; oh, Babs, year after year until I am old— an old, old woman with grey hair and a wizened face, left alone, with no one to care for me! Oh, yes, yes, I know what you would say, but father and mother will be dead, and you will be married in a home of your own, and Spencer very likely at the other end of the world, and—"

"And Jim?" I asked quietly.

"Ah, poor Jim! He must marry, too; it isn't fair to let him wreck his life. He does love me, poor fellow, but no one else does nowadays. Men don't like invalids. They are sorry for them, and pity them. Will Dudley, for instance—he only comes to see me as a charity—because I am ill, and need amusing—"

"He is engaged to another girl, Vere. Surely you don't want him to come for love?"

She flushed a little, but her face set in the old defiant fashion, and she said obstinately—

"He would have loved me if I had been well! Rachel Greaves will never satisfy him. He cares for her as a sister rather than as a wife. If I were well again, and gay and bright as I used to be—"

"He would care for you less than he does now. You don't understand, Vere; but I am certain that Mr Dudley will never desert Rachel for another girl. He may not be passionately in love with her, perhaps it is not his nature to be demonstrative, but he has an intense admiration for her character, and would rather die than disappoint her in any way."

"You seem to know a great deal about it. How can you be sure that you understand him better than I do?" she asked sharply, and I could only say in reply—

"I don't know; but I *am* sure! I think one understands some people by instinct, and he and I were friends from the moment we met. Besides, I know Rachel better than you do, and had more opportunity of watching her life at home. I say her life, but she has practically no life of her own—it is entirely given up for others. Think what she gives up, Vere! She could have been married years ago, and had a happy home of her own, but she won't leave her father, though he is so cross and disagreeable that most people would be thankful to get away. She has the dullest, most monotonous time one can imagine, and hardly ever sees Will alone; but she is quite happy—not resigned, not forbearing nor any pretence like that, but really and truly and honestly happy. I call it splendid! There are lots of people in the world who have hard things to bear, and who bear them bravely enough, but they are not *happy* in doing it. Rachel is—that's the wonderful thing about her!"

"I wonder if she could make me happy. I wonder if she could tell me how to like lying here!" said poor Vere with a sob, and the idea must have grown in her mind, for a week after our return home she said suddenly, "I want to see Rachel Greaves!" and nothing would satisfy her but that she must be invited forthwith.

Rachel came. I had not seen her for some months, and I thought she looked thin and pale.

As we went upstairs together our two figures were reflected in the big mirror on the first landing—one all grey and brown, the other all white, and pink, and gold. I felt ashamed and uncomfortable at the contrast in our appearance, but Rachel didn't; not a bit! She just looked round at me, and beamed in the sweetest way, and said—

"You are more like a flower than ever, Una! It *is* nice to see you again!" and she meant it, every word. She really is too good to live!

I took her to Vere's room, and was going to leave them alone, but Vere called me back, and made me stay. She said afterwards that she wanted me to hear what was said, so that I could remind her of anything which she forgot. There was only half an hour before tea, so Vere lost no time in stupid trivialities.

"I sent for you to come to see me, Rachel, because I wanted particularly to ask you a question. I have been ill nearly a year now, and I get no better. I am beginning to fear I shall never get better, but have to be like this all my life. I have lain here with that thought to keep me company until I can bear it no longer. I feel sometimes as if I am going out of my senses. I must find something to help me, or it may really come to that in the end. I keep up pretty well during the day, for I hate being pitied, and that keeps me from breaking down in public; but the nights—the long, long endless nights! Nobody knows what I endure in the nights! You are so good—everyone says you are so good—tell me how to bear it and not mind! Tell me what I am to do to grow patient and resigned!"

"Dear Vere, I have never been tried as you are. I have had only one or two short illnesses in my life—I have never known the weariness and disappointment—"

"No, but you have other trials. You have so much to bear, and it is so dull and wretched for you all the time," interrupted Vere quickly, too much engrossed in her own affairs to realise that it was not the most polite thing in the world to denounce another girl's surroundings. As for Rachel, she opened her eyes in purest amazement that anyone should imagine she needed pity.

"I? Oh, you are mistaken—quite, quite mistaken. I have the most happy home. Everyone is good and kind to me; I have no troubles, except seeing dear father's sufferings; and so many blessings—so much to be thankful for!"

"You mean your engagement? Mr Dudley is charming, and I am sure you are fond of him, but you can't be married while your father lives, and—and—one never knows what may happen. Suppose— changes came—"

Vere stopped short in the middle of her sentence, and, by a curious impulse, Rachel turned suddenly and looked at me. Our eyes met, and the expression in hers—the piteous, shrinking look—made me rush hotly into the breach.

"You are talking nonsense, Vere! You don't know Mr Dudley as Rachel does. You don't understand his character."

"No," said Rachel proudly, "you don't understand. It is quite possible that we may never marry—many things might happen to prevent that, but Will would never do anything that was mean and unworthy. The changes, whatever they were, could not affect my love for him, and it is that that makes my happiness—"

"Loving him! Not his loving you! Rachel, are you sure?"

"Oh, quite sure. Think just for a moment, and you will see that it must be so. It is pleasant to be loved, but if you do not love in return you must still feel lonely and dissatisfied at heart. If you love, you care so much, so very, very much for the other's welfare, that there is simply no time left to remember yourself; or, if you did, what does it matter? What would anything matter so long as he were well and happy?"

Her face glowed with earnestness and enthusiasm—what a contrast from Vere's fretful, restless expression, which always seems asking for something more, something she has not got, something she cannot even understand. Even Vere realised the difference, and her fingers closed over Rachel's hand with an eloquent pressure. Vere never does things by halves, and even her apologies are graceful and pretty.

"Ah, Rachel," she said, "I see how foolish I was to expect you to answer my question in a few short words. We speak different languages, you and I, and I can't even understand your meaning. I wish I could, Rachel—I wish I could! The old life is out of reach, and there is nothing left to take its place. Can't you teach me your secret to help me along?"

Rachel flushed all over her face and neck. Now that she was asked a direct question she was obliged to answer, but her voice was very shy and quiet, as if the subject were almost too sacred to be discussed.

"I think the secret lies in the way we look at life—whether we want our own way, or are content to accept what God sends. If we love and trust Him, we know that what He chooses must be best, and with that knowledge comes rest, and the end of the struggle—"

"Ah," sighed Vere, "but it's not the end with me! I believe it, too, with my head, but when the pain comes on, and the sleepless nights, and the unbearable restlessness that is worst of all—I forget! I can't rest, I *can't* trust, it is all blackness and darkness. I must be very wicked, for even when I try hardest I fail."

"Dear Vere," said Rachel softly, "don't be too hard on yourself! When people are tired and worn with suffering they are not responsible for all they say and do. I know that with my own dear father. When he is cross and unreasonable we are not angry, we understand and pity, and try to comfort him, and if we feel like that, poor imperfect creatures as we are, what must God be, Who is the very heart of love! He is your kindest judge, dear, for He knows how hard it is to bear."

"Thank you!" whispered Vere brokenly. She put her hand up to her face, and I could see her tremble. She could not bear any more agitation just then, so I signalled to Rachel, and we gradually turned the conversation to ordinary topics.

Eventually Will arrived, and we had tea and some rather strained small talk, for Vere was quiet and absent-minded, and somehow or other Will rarely speaks to me directly nowadays. He is always perfectly nice and polite, but he does avoid me. I don't think he likes me half as much as he did at first.

How suddenly things happen in life! At the moment when you expect it least, the scene changes, and the whole future is changed. As we were sipping our tea and eating cakes, Burrows, the parlourmaid, opened the door, and announced in her usual expressionless voice—

"If you please, marm, a messenger has come to request Miss Greaves to return home at once. Mr Greaves has had a sudden stroke—"

We all stood up quickly, all save poor Vere, who has to be still whatever happens. Rachel turned very white, and Will went up to her, and took her hand in his. He looked at me, and I guessed what he meant, and said quickly—

"The motor-car! It shall come round at once, and you will be home in five minutes. I'll go round to the stables!"

I rushed off, thankful to be able to help, and to put off thinking as long as possible, but even as I ran the thought flew through my head. A stroke! That was serious—very serious in Mr Greaves's weakened condition. I could tell from Burrows' manner that the message had been urgent. Perhaps even now the end of the long suffering *was* at hand—the end of something else, too; of what had seemed an hour ago a practically hopeless engagement!

Chapter Twenty One.

August 12th.

It is a long time since I opened this diary, for I have grown out of the habit of writing, and it is difficult to get into it again.

Mr Greaves died the very night of his seizure, and immediately after his funeral Mrs Greaves collapsed and has been an invalid ever since. It seemed as if she had kept up to the very limit of her endurance, for as soon as the strain was over her nerves gave way in a rush, and instead of the gentle, self-controlled creature which she has been all her life, she is now just a bundle of fancies, tears and repinings. It is hard on Rachel, but she bears it like an angel, and is always patient and amiable. I wondered at first if she and Will would marry soon and take Mrs Greaves to live with them; I asked Rachel about it one day when we were having a quiet chat, and she answered quite openly:

"Will wished it. He thought he could help me to cheer mother, but she won't hear of it for the next twelve months at least, and, of course, I must do as she prefers. We have waited so long that another year cannot make much difference."

I wondered if Will were of the same opinion, but did not dare to ask him. As I said before, he avoids me nowadays and does not seem to care to talk to me alone. Perhaps it is better so, but I can't help being sorry. I have wondered sometimes if the dull, aching feeling which I have when he passes me by is anything like what poor Wallace Forbes felt about me. If it is, I am even more sorry for Wallace than before. Of course, I am not in love with Will—I couldn't be, for he is engaged to Rachel, and I have known it from the first, but I can't help thinking about him, and watching for him, and feeling happy if he comes, and wretched if he stays away. And I know his face by heart and just how it looks on every occasion. His eyes don't twinkle nearly so much as they did; he is graver altogether, except sometimes when I have a mad mood and set myself to make him frisky too. I can always succeed, but I don't try often, for I fancy Rachel doesn't like it. She can't frisk herself, poor dear, and it must feel horrid to feel left out in the cold by your very own *fiancé*. I should hate it myself.

At the beginning of this month I had a great treat. Lorna came to stay with me for three days. She was visiting a friend twenty miles off, and came here in the middle of her visit just for that short time, so that there need be no necessity for Wallace to know anything about it. Of course, she came with her parents' consent and approval, and oh, how thankful I was to see her and to look upon her coming as a sign that they were beginning to forgive me. Of course we talked shoals about Wallace, for I just longed to know how he was faring.

"My dear, it was awful after you left—positively awful!" Lorna said. "Wallace went about looking like a ghost, and mother cried, and father was worried to death. Wallace declared at first that he would go abroad, but father told him that it was cowardly to throw up his work for the sake of a disappointment, however bitter, and mother asked if he really cared so little for his parents that he could forsake them in their old age for the sake of a girl whom he had only known a month. He gave way at last, as I knew he would, and set to work harder than ever. He was very brave, poor old boy, and never broke down nor made any fuss, but he was so silent! You would not have known him. He never seemed to laugh, nor to joke, nor take any interest in what was going on, and the whole winter long he never once entered my little den, where we had had such happy times. I suppose it reminded him too much of you. This spring, however, he has been brighter. I insisted on his taking me to the tennis club as usual, and though he went at first for my sake he enjoys it now for his own. We meet so many friends, and he can't help being happy out in the sunshine with a lot of happy boys and girls all round. He was quite keen about the tournament, and had such a pretty partner. He always walked home with her after the matches."

"How nice!" I said, and tried to be pleased and relieved, and succeeded only in feeling irritated and rubbed the wrong way. How mean it sounds! How selfish, and small, and contemptible! I just intend to *make* myself feel glad, and to hope that Wallace may see more and more of that pretty girl, and like her far better than me, and be right down thankful that I refused him. So now, Una Sackville, you know what is expected of you!

Vere liked Lorna, and was amused to see us frisking about together. The afternoon before Lorna left we were chasing each other round the room in some mad freak when, turning towards Vere's couch, I thought I saw her head raised an inch or so from the pillow in her effort to follow our movements. My heart gave a great thud of excitement, but I couldn't be sure, so I took no notice, but took care to retire still further into the corner. Then I looked round again, and, yes! it was perfectly true, her head was a good three inches from the couch, and she was smiling all the time, evidently quite free from pain.

"Oh, Vere!" I cried; "oh, darling, darling Vere!" and suddenly the tears rolled down my cheeks, and I trembled so that I could hardly stand. Lorna could not think what had happened, neither could Vere herself, and I tried hard to calm myself so as not to excite her too much.

"You raised your head, Vere! Oh, ever so high you raised it! You were watching us, and forgot all about yourself, and it didn't hurt you a bit—you smiled all the time. Try again if you don't believe me—try, darling. You can do it, if you like!"

Her breath came short with nervousness and agitation, but she clenched her hands and with a sudden effort her head and neck lifted themselves one, two, a good three or four inches from their support. Oh, her face! The sight of it at that moment was almost enough to make up for those long months of anxiety. It was illuminated; it shone! All the weary lines and hollows disappeared, the colour rushed to her cheeks; it was the old, lovely, radiant Vere, whom we had thought never to see again.

I can't describe what we did next. Mother came in and cried, father came in and clapped his hands, and asked mother what on earth she meant by crying, while the tears were rolling down his own dear old nose in the most barefaced manner all the time. I danced about the house and kissed everyone I met, and the servants cried and laughed, and the old family doctor was sent for and came in beaming and rubbing his hands with delight. He said it was a wonderful improvement, and the best possible augury of complete recovery, and that now the first step had been taken we could look forward to continuous improvement.

Oh, how happy we were! I don't think any of us slept much that night; we just lay awake and thanked God, and gloated over the glad news. All the next day Vere's face shone with the same wonderful incredulous joy. Hope had been very nearly dead for the last few months, and the sudden change from despair to practical certainty was too great to realise. It seemed as if she did not know how to be thankful enough. She said to me once—

"I am going to get well, Babs, but I must never forget this experience! As long as I live I shall keep this couch in my bedroom, and when I have been selfish and worldly I shall lay down straight on my back as I have done all these months and stay there for an hour or two, just to make myself remember how much I have been spared, and how humble I ought to be. And if you ever see me forgetting and going back to the old thoughtless ways, you must remind me, Babs; you must speak straight out and stop me in time. I want to look back on this illness and feel that it has been the turning-point in my life."

Later on the same day she said suddenly—

"I want Jim! Please send for Jim." And when he came, rushing on the wings of the express next day, she was so sweet and kind to him that the poor fellow did not know whether he was standing on his head or his heels.

It was characteristic of Jim that when recovery seemed certain he should say no more about his own hopes. He had been anxious enough to offer his love in the dark days of uncertainty, and all the year long a day had never passed without bringing Vere some sign of his remembrance—a letter, or a book, or a magazine, or flowers, or scent, or chocolates. The second post never once came in without bringing a message of love and cheer. He came down to see us, too, once a month at least, and sometimes got very little thanks for his pains, but that made no difference to his devotion. Now for the first time he was silent and said not one word of love.

Vere told me all about it afterwards, not the nice private little bits, of course, but a general outline of the scene between them, and I could imagine how pretty it must have been. Vere is bewitching when she is saucy, and it is, oh, so good to see her saucy again!

"There sat Jim like a monument of propriety," she said, dimpling with amusement at the remembrance, "and do what I would I could not get him on to personal topics. I gave him half a dozen leads, but the wretch always drifted on to the weather, or politics, or books, and I could not corner him. Then at last I said mournfully, 'Haven't you brought me a *cadeau*, Jim? I looked forward to a *cadeau*. Is there nothing you want to give me?' He apologised profusely, said there had been no time before catching the train, but if there was anything at all that I fancied when he went back to town he would be only too charmed. I looked down and twiddled my fingers, and said bashfully, 'Well, Jim, I should like—a ring—!'"

Dear old Jim! Dear old loyal, faithful Jim! How I should have loved to see his face at that moment!

Chapter Twenty Two.

September 5th.

Every day Vere seems to improve. It is simply wonderful how she has bounded ahead after the first start. Hope and happiness have a great deal to do with it, the doctor says, and the expectation of being better, which has taken the place of the old despair. She looks deliciously happy, and satisfied, and at rest, while as for Jim—he is ten years younger at the very least, and can hardly believe that his good fortune is true, and not a dream.

Needless to say he bought the ring at once—such a beauty! A great big pearl surrounded with diamonds. I mean to have the twin of it when I am engaged myself. Vere wears it hung on a chain round her neck for the present, but as soon as she can walk it is to go on her finger, and the engagement will be announced. She has been propped up on her couch higher and higher every day, and yesterday she actually sat on a chair for half an hour, and felt none the worse.

We are all so happy that we don't know what to do—at least, I am miserable enough sometimes when I am alone, and begin thinking of myself. When Vere marries and goes away I shall be horribly dull, and when Rachel marries I wonder where they will live—the Dudleys, I mean! *The Dudleys!* Will is heir to an old bachelor uncle who has a place in the North. That's the reason why he is learning to be an agent here, so that he may know how to manage his own land when he gets it. I think, on the whole, I would rather he and Rachel went quite away, but how flat and uninteresting everything would be! I shall have to go about with father more than ever, but we shall never meet Will striding about in his tweed suit and deerstalker cap; he will never join us any more and have nice long talks. Oh, dear! Why do people want to marry other people in this world? Why can't they all go on as they are, being friends and having a good time together? Captain Grantly married Lady Mary at Easter, and I suppose Wallace will marry the pretty girl next, and Lorna will write to say she is engaged, and can't be bothered with me any more.

I shall never marry. I could never induce myself to accept a second-best as Vere has done. That sounds horrid, and, of course, she declares now that she never cared for another man, but I know better! She was in love with Will at one time, but she knew it was hopeless, and Jim's devotion during all those weary months was enough to melt a heart of stone.

Vere wished Rachel to be told of her engagement at once, and despatched me to the Grange to carry the news, and, as Will Dudley happened to be there at the time, he was really obliged to walk home with me, so far, at least, as our paths lay together. It was the first time we had been really alone for an age, and we were both rather silent for the first part of the walk. Then we began talking of the engagement, and got on better. Will had been a little uncertain in his congratulations, and he explained why.

"Carstairs is a splendid fellow. I admire him immensely, and there is no doubt about his feelings. He has adored your sister for years, but—she never appeared to me to appreciate his devotion!"

I smiled to myself, recalling Vere's rhapsodies of an hour ago.

"By her own account she has never thought of anyone else, nor cared for anyone else, nor wished for anyone else, but has adored him all the time she was snubbing him and flirting with other men. Curious, isn't it? The funny part of it is she really and truly believes that it is true."

"For the moment—yes. I can understand that. She is altogether in a highly nervous, exalted condition, and feels that the first act of convalescence ought to be to reward his long waiting. My only fear is that when she gets back to a normal condition she may realise that what she feels is more gratitude and affection than love."

"I don't think so, and you wouldn't either if you saw them together. I detest lovers as a rule, they are so dull and self-engrossed; but it is pretty to watch Vere and Jim. She is so saucy and domineering, and he is so blissfully happy to be bullied. Oh, yes, I am sure it is all right! I am sure they will be happy."

"God grant it!" he said solemnly. "Everything depends upon the truth of their feelings for each other. If that is right, nothing else will have power to hurt them seriously. If it is not—" He broke off, looking so serious that I felt frightened, and said nervously:

"But, surely—even at the worst, gratitude and affection would be a good foundation!"

"For everything else, but not for marriage. It is a ghastly mistake to imagine that they can ever take the place of love. Never fall into that error, Babs, however much you may be tempted. Never let any impulse of gratitude or pity induce you to promise to marry a man if you have no warmer feeling. It would be the most cruel thing you could do, not only for yourself, but for him!"

"I have fallen into it once already, but he would not have me," I said, recalling my hasty speech to Wallace Forbes, and at that Will's face lit up with sudden animation, and he cried eagerly:

"Was that the explanation? I guessed, of course, that something had happened while you were away last autumn. You remember I was calling on your sister at the time of your unexpected return, and you have never been quite the same since? Whatever happened then has changed you from a girl into a woman."

I sighed, as I always did when I recalled that miserable incident.

"I am glad you think so. I want to be changed. Please don't think me the heroine of an interesting romance. I was a selfish wretch, and amused myself by flirting without thinking of anything but my own amusement. I was very down on my luck just then, and had got it into my head that no one cared for me, and when—he—*did*, it

152

cheered and soothed my feelings, so I let things drift until it was too late. Do you despise me altogether, or can you understand that, bad as it was, it wasn't so hopelessly bad as it sounds?"

"I understand better than you think, perhaps. And you repented in sackcloth and ashes, and were ready to make a sacrifice of yourself by way of reparation? Thank heaven he was man enough to refuse that offer! Whatever happens to the rest of us, you, at least, must be happy. You were meant for happiness, and must not throw it aside. I shall probably leave this place soon, and we may seldom meet in the future, but I should like to think of you in the sunshine. Promise me to be happy, Babs! Promise me that you will be happy!"

He turned towards me with a violence of voice and manner so unlike his usual composed, half-quizzical manner, that I was quite aghast, and did not know how to reply. For the first time a doubt of his own happiness sprang into my mind, and once there it seemed to grow bigger and bigger with every moment that passed. He did not speak like a happy man; he did not look like a man whose heart was at rest. Looking at him closely, I saw a network of lines about his mouth, which I had never noticed before; his eyes looked tired and sunken. He has changed since I saw him first a year ago, and yet there seems nothing to account for it, for his circumstances are all the same. Is he depressed because Rachel still puts off their marriage? Oh, if I were in her place I could not endure to see him looking ill and sad, and still leave him alone! Nothing should keep me away! I'd jump over the moon to get to his side!

We stood still in the middle of the quiet path and stared at each other. I don't know what he was thinking, but my own thoughts made me blush and change the subject hurriedly.

"Oh, I mean to be happy! I have had so much anxiety and trouble this last year that I'm just bubbling over with pent-up spirits. This engagement has put the finishing touch to my self-control, and I must do something at once to let off steam. Did you hear me ask Rachel to go over to Farnham with us to-morrow? Father and mother and I are going to do it in record time in the new motor, and Rachel is coming, too. She has never been in a motor, and is eager to see what it is like. It's quite a triumph to get her to accept an invitation, isn't it? You can come, too, if you like; there's room for another, and the more the merrier. Do come, and let us all be happy together! We could have such a merry day!"

He hesitated for a moment, then laughed in a sort of reckless way, and cried loudly:

"Yes, let us be happy! It is only for one day. Let us throw care to the winds, and think of nothing but our own enjoyment. Oh, yes, I'll come! We will have a happy day, Babs—a happy day together!"

So now it is all arranged, and I am longing for the time to come. We three will sit together on the back seat and talk all the time, and, as Will says, I shall just forget everything in the world I don't care to remember, and enjoy every minute of the time.

Chapter Twenty Three.

September 6th, 11 PM.

Here I am back in my own room; at least, I suppose it is me. I have been staring at myself in the glass, and I look much the same. No one who didn't know would guess what had happened to me during the last few hours, and that to myself I feel all new and strange—a Una Sackville who was never really alive until to-day.

I ought to be desperately miserable, and I am, but I am happy, too; half the time I am so happy that I forget all about the past and the future, and remember only the present. To-morrow morning, I suppose, I shall begin worrying and fighting against fate, but for to-night I am content—so utterly, perfectly content that there is no room to want anything more. I'll begin at the beginning, and tell it straight through to the end.

We started off for our ride at twelve o'clock this morning in the highest of spirits, for the sun was shining, the sky was a deep cloudless blue, and, better than all, Vere had taken her first walk across the floor, supported by father on one side, and Jim on the other, and had managed far better than any of us had expected. She and Jim had arranged to have lunch together in the garden, and she waved her hand to us at parting, and cried airily:

"Perhaps I may stroll down to the Lodge to meet you on your return!"

Father and mother looked at one another when they were outside the door, so happy, poor dears, that they hardly knew whether to laugh or to cry, and then out we went into the sunshine, where the motor was throbbing and bumping as if it were impatient to be off. When I invent a motor I'll make one that can be quiet when it stands. I'm not a bit nervous when once we are started, but I hate it while we are waiting, and the stupid thing behaves as if it were going to blow up every moment.

Rachel was waiting for us, and flushed to the loveliest pink when Will appeared and she discovered that he was to be one of the party. Father, mother and the chauffeur sat on the front seat, Rachel and I on the one behind, with Will in the middle, and the luncheon-baskets were packed away behind. I had a mad turn, and was quite "fey," as the Scotch say. I kept them laughing the whole time, and was quite surprised at my own wit. It seemed as if someone else was talking through my lips, for I said the things almost before I thought of them.

We rushed along through beautiful country lanes, through dear, sleepy little villages, and along the banks of the river. The motor behaved beautifully, and neither smelt nor shook; it was quite intoxicating to fly through the air without any feeling of exertion, and Rachel herself grew almost frisky in time.

At two o'clock we camped out, and had a delicious luncheon; then off we started again, to take a further circuit of the country, and have tea at a quaint old inn on the way home. All went well until about four o'clock, when we began to descend a long, steep hill leading to a riverside village. Father told the chauffeur to take it as slowly as possible, but we had not covered a quarter of the way when— something happened! Suddenly, without the slightest warning, the machine seemed to leap forward like an arrow from a bow, and rush down the hill, more and more quickly with every second that passed. We all called out in alarm, and the chauffeur turned a bleached face to father, and said shakily:

"It's gone, sir! The brake has gone. I can't hold her!"

"Gone? Broken? Are you sure—perfectly sure?"

"Quite sure, sir. What shall I do? Run through the village and chance the river, or turn up the bank?"

We knew the village—one long, narrow street crowded with excursionists, with vehicles of all descriptions, with little children playing about. At the end the road gave a sharp turn close to the water's edge. On the other hand the bank was high and steep, and in some places covered with flints.

Father looked round, and his face whitened, but he said firmly:

"We will not risk other lives besides our own. If that is the choice, run her up the bank, Johnson!"

"Right, sir!" said the chauffeur.

It all happened in a moment, but it seemed like hours and hours. The machine shook and quivered, and turned unwillingly to the side. The bank seemed to rush at us—to grow steeper and steeper; to tower above our heads like a mountain. My heart seemed to stop beating; a far-away voice said clearly in my brain, "*This is death!*" and a great wave of despair rolled over me. I turned instinctively towards Will, and at the same moment he turned towards me, and his eyes were bright and shining.

"Una, Una!" he cried, and his arms opened wide and clasped me in a tight, protecting embrace. There was a crash and a roar, a feeling of mounting upwards to the skies, and then—darkness!

The next thing was waking up feeling heavy and dazed, staring stupidly at my coat-sleeve, and wondering what it was, and how I came to be wearing such an extraordinary night-gown. Then I tried to move the arm, and it was heavy and painful; and suddenly I remembered! I was not dead at all, not even, it appeared, seriously hurt. But the others? I sat up and glanced fearfully around. The motor lay half-way up the bank, a shattered mass. Father was on his knees beside mother, who was moaning in a low, unconscious fashion. Will was slowly scrambling to his feet, holding one hand to his back. Rachel lay white and still as death, but her eyes were open, and she was evidently fully conscious. The chauffeur was dreadful to look at, with the blood pouring from his head, but he, too, moaned, and moved his limbs. Nobody was dead! It was almost too wonderful to be believed. I dragged myself across to mother, and she opened her eyes and smiled faintly at the sight of our anxious faces. Her dear hands were terribly cut; she winced with pain as she sat up, and was evidently badly bruised, but it was such bliss to see her move and hear her speak that these seemed but light things. Father rushed to the motor, managed to extricate a flask from the scattered contents, and went round administering doses of brandy to us all in turns. He had ricked his knee, and hobbled about like an old man. Will had a bad pain in his back, and a cut on his forehead. My left arm was useless. Rachel seemed utterly stunned, and unable to speak or move, and the poor chauffeur was unconscious, having fallen on his head on a mass of flints.

By this time the accident had become known, and the village people came trooping up the hill, bringing stretchers with them, for, as they afterwards explained, they expected to find us all dead. The chauffeur and Rachel were carried in front, but the rest of us preferred to hobble along on our own feet, mother leaning on father's arm, Will and I, one on each side, never once glancing in the other's face. It was awful to be alive, and to remember that last moment when we had forgotten everything in the world but our two selves. I felt like a murderess when I looked at Rachel's still face, and hated myself for what I had done. Yet how could I help it? When you face death at the distance of a few seconds, all pretence dies away, and you act unconsciously as the heart dictates. I wanted Will— and—*Will wanted me!* Oh, it is wonderful, wonderful to think of! All these months when he has avoided me, and I thought he liked me less, has he really been loving me, and trying to get over it in loyalty to poor, dear Rachel? And was that what it meant when he called me "Una!" and his voice lingered over the word?

Looking back now, I can understand lots of things which puzzled and worried me at the time. I think he began to love me almost at the very first, as I did him. But oh, Rachel, Rachel—dear, sweet, unselfish Rachel! I'd rather die than steal your happiness from you! Did she hear, I wonder? Did she *see*? Father and mother were too much engrossed in themselves to know anything about it—perhaps she, too, was too excited to notice. Yet, surely in that awful moment she would turn to Will for comfort, and when she saw him absorbed in me, forgetting her very existence, she must understand. Oh, she must!

I was terrified to meet her eyes when at last we reached the parlour of the inn, and the doctor came to attend to us all in turns. She was lying on the sofa, and when I made myself go over to speak to her, my heart gave a great throb of thankfulness, for she smiled at me, very feebly, but as sweetly as ever, and pressed my hand between hers. She shook her head when I asked her a question, and seemed as if she could not bear to talk. The doctor was puzzled by her condition; he could find no real injuries, but said she was evidently suffering from shock, and must be kept as quiet as possible until she recovered her nerve. We were sponged, bandaged, plastered, and fortified with tea, and a wretched livid-looking party we were! No one could possibly have recognised us as the same people who had set out so gaily four hours before.

The doctor was anxious that we should telegraph home, and spend the night at the inn, but we had two more invalids to consider—Mrs Greaves and Vere, neither of whom were fit to be left alone in suspense, so we chartered a big covered omnibus, borrowed dozens of pillows and cushions, and set out to drive the remaining ten miles, leaving the chauffeur to be taken to the village hospital. Mother, Rachel and I lay full length along the seats, the two men banked themselves up with pillows, and endured the shaking as best they could, and so at last we reached our separate homes. I have been sitting here by my desk thinking, thinking, thinking for over an hour, and it all comes to the same thing.

I have made one man unhappy through my selfish vanity; I will not ruin a woman's life into the bargain. Rachel is my friend, and I will be truly and utterly loyal to her. So far my conscience is clear of offence where she is concerned, for if I have loved Will it has been unconsciously, and without realising what I was doing. I have never, never tried to attract him nor take him from her in any way. I have looked upon him as much out of my reach as if he had been a married man, but after this things will be different. I know the danger that is before us both, and shall have to watch myself sternly every minute of the time.

I suppose I shall be an old maid now, for I can't imagine caring for anyone after Will. Father and mother will be glad, and I'll try to be a comfort to them, but it will be dreadful getting old, and ugly, and tired and ill, and never having a real home of my own, and someone to like me *best*. Preachey people would say that it is wrong of me to want to be first, and that I should be quite content to take a lower place, but I can't think that can be true where love is concerned, else why did God put this longing in women's hearts? Anyway, I've found out that love — the *best* kind of love — is His gift, and if it comes to me at all it shall *be* as His gift. I won't steal it! Poor, darling, unselfish Rachel, for your sake I must guard my thoughts as well as my deeds.

I think perhaps I'd better not write any more in this diary for a time. It would be difficult to write of just ordinary things without referring to the one great subject, and that is just what I must not do. My business is to forget, not to remember. I must not allow myself to think!

Chapter Twenty Four.

January 1st.

I must begin to write again in my poor, neglected diary, for things are happening so fast that if I do not keep a record of them as they pass I shall forget half that I want to remember.

The last entry was written on the evening after the motor accident, nearly four months ago, so I must go back to that day and tell what happened in the interval.

We were all invalided more or less for a few weeks, but providentially there were no serious developments; even the poor chauffeur recovered and seemed as well as ever. Rachel was the longest in gaining strength, and the doctor was worried about her, for she seemed listless and uninterested in what was going on, so different from her usual happy self. He said she had evidently had a severe nervous shock, and that that sort of thing was often more difficult to overcome than more tangible injuries. A nurse came down from London to look after her and her mother, and finally they went off to Bournemouth, where they intend to remain until the worst of the winter is over.

I was relieved to feel convinced that Rachel knew nothing of what had occurred at that last dreadful moment, for her ignorance seemed proved by the fact that she was absolutely the same in manner both to Will and myself! in fact, if anything, I think she was more affectionate to me than she had ever been before. I *was* thankful! It would have been dreadful to feel that we had any part in bringing about her illness. As for Will, I kept carefully out of his way, and hoped we need never, never refer to what had passed; but he evidently felt differently, and one day when he knew where I was bound he deliberately waylaid me and had it out. I never lifted my eyes from the ground, so I don't know how he looked, but his voice told plainly enough how agitated he was feeling.

"There is something I have to say, and the sooner it is said the better for both of us," he began. "I owe you an explanation for what occurred—that day. I should like you to understand that I hardly knew what I was about. It seemed as if it might be the last moment of life, and I turned instinctively to you. Otherwise I would never, never—"

"Oh, I know!" I cried brokenly. "I understand it all, and if there is any blame it is mine as much as yours, for I forgot, too. We must never refer to it again, and we had better see each other as seldom as possible. It will be easier that way."

He was silent for a moment or two, then he sighed heavily and said:

"It will not be easy any way, Una, but it must be done. I can't blame myself altogether for what has happened. Our hearts are not always in our own keeping, and mine went out to you from the first. I did not realise it for a time, but when I did, I did not trifle with temptation. I kept out of your way, as you must have noticed. All last winter I fought a hard fight. It would have been harder still if I had guessed that—you cared! The trouble began in mistaking friendship for love, but until I met you I was quite content. I had no idea that anything was lacking."

"And you will be happy again. Rachel is better than I am in every possible way, and is more worthy of you. I am a selfish, discontented wretch. If you knew what I was really like, you would wonder how you could ever have cared for me at all, and when you leave this place it will be easy to forget—"

"I shall never forget," he said shortly. "Una, I must tell you all that is in my mind. I believe in honesty in love as in all other matters, and if circumstances were different I should go straight to Rachel and tell her. How, unconsciously to myself, my heart had gone out to you, and that in that supreme moment we turned instinctively to each other, and I knew that my love was returned, and I would ask her for my liberty. In nine out of ten cases I am sure that would be the right thing to do, but—this is the tenth! Rachel has had years of trouble

162

and anxiety, and now her own health is broken. I could not put another burden upon her. Through these last days of misery and uncertainty what has comforted me most has been to realise that she has no idea of what happened. She must have been taken up with her own thoughts—praying, no doubt, for our safety, not her own. Rachel never thinks of herself, so I must think for her. With her father gone, her mother invalided, she has no one left but me, and I can't desert her."

"I should hate you if you did!" I cried eagerly. "I, too, have been thankful that she knows nothing, and she must never know, you must never let her guess. There could be no happiness for us if we broke her heart. You used to call her the best woman in the world, and she is so sweet and gentle that you could not possibly live with her and remain unhappy. In years to come you will be thankful it has happened like this."

"In any case it is the right thing to do," he said, sighing. "As you say, we should only suffer if we thought of ourselves first. If one tries to grasp happiness at the expense of another's suffering it only collapses like a bubble, and leaves one more wretched than before. You and I are not unprincipled, Una, though we did forget ourselves for that one moment, and the remembrance of Rachel would poison everything. Perhaps, after all, it is as well that we know our danger, for we shall be more careful to keep out of temptation. I shall try to persuade her to marry me as soon as possible, and after that we shall live near my uncle. I shall have a busy, active life, and, as you say, one of the sweetest women in the world for my wife. She has been faithful to me for so many years that I should be a scoundrel if I did not make her happy."

I did not say anything—I couldn't! I seemed to see it all stretched out before me—Will being married, and going to live far, far away, and settling down with his wife and children, and forgetting that there was a Una in the world. I tried to be glad at the thought; I tried *hard*, but I was just one big ache, and my heart felt as if it would burst. Honestly and truly, if by lifting up a little finger at that moment I could have hindered their happiness, nothing would have induced me to do it, but it is difficult to do right *cheerfully*.

We stood silently for a long time, until Will said brokenly: "And what will—you do, Una?"

"Oh, I shall do nothing. I shall stay at home—like the little pig," I said, trying to laugh, and succeeding very badly. "I shall help Vere with her marriage preparations, and visit her in her new home, and take care of the parents in their old age. Father says there ought always to be one unmarried woman in every family to play Aunt Mary in time of need. I shall be the Sackville Aunt Mary."

He turned and walked up and down the path. I stole a glance at him and saw that he was battling with some strong emotion, then our eyes met, and he came forward hastily and stood before me.

"Oh, it is hard that I should have brought this upon you! I who would give my right hand to ensure your happiness. Have I spoilt your life, Una? Will you think hardly of me some day, and wish that we had never met?"

Then at last I looked full in his face.

"No, Will," I said; "that day will never come. I have known a good man, and I am proud that he has loved me, and prouder still that he is true to his word. Don't worry about me. I shall try to be happy and brave, and make the most of my life. It will be easier after you have left. We must not meet like this again. I could not bear that."

"No, we must not meet. I could not bear it either, but I am glad that we have spoken out this once. God bless you, dear, for your sweet words. They will be a comfort to remember. Good-bye!"

We did not even shake hands; he just took off his cap and—went! I had a horrible impulse to run after him, take him by the arm, and make him stay a little longer, only five minutes longer, but I didn't. I just stood perfectly still and heard his footsteps crunch down the path. Then the sound died away, and it seemed as if everything else died with them. I did not feel brave at that moment. There seemed nothing left in the whole wide world that was worth having.

Chapter Twenty Five.

About the middle of September Will went away to pay a visit to his uncle. He called to say good-bye when he knew I was out, so we did not meet again, and no one had any idea of what had happened. Isn't it strange how far away you feel at times from even your nearest relations?

"Not e'en the dearest heart and next our own,
Knows half the reason why we smile or sigh!"

as it says in the "Christian Year." A girl's parents think: "She has a comfortable home, and nice food and clothes, and we are always thinking of her; she ought to be happy, and if she isn't she is a naughty, ungrateful child!" They don't remember that the child is a woman, and wants her very own life! And other people say: "She is a well-off girl, that Una Sackville, she has everything that money can buy!" but money can't take the ache out of your heart. And your sister thinks that you should be so excited and eager at the prospect of being her bridesmaid, that your cup of happiness ought to simply pour over on the spot. Ah, well, perhaps it's just as well to keep your troubles to yourself!

The old uncle was weak and failing, so Will stayed on with him until Christmas. I suppose he was glad of the excuse. He never wrote, but Rachel sent me a note now and then, and mentioned that he had been down to Bournemouth several times, but she is a poor correspondent at the best of times, and her letters seemed emptier than ever. When Lorna writes, you feel as if she were speaking, and she tells you all the nice, interesting little things you most want to hear, but Rachel's letters are just a dull repetition of your own.

"Dearest Una,—I am so glad to hear you are keeping well, and feeling happier about your sister's health. It is very nice to know that dear Mrs Sackville is so much stronger this winter, and that your father is full of health and vigour. So you are expecting a visit from your soldier brother, and are all greatly excited at the prospect of seeing him after so many years, etcetera, etcetera, etcetera." What is one to do with people who write like that? Just at the end she would say, "Will paid us a flying visit last week, and promised to come again next Saturday. Believe me, dear Una..." Her letters left me as hungry and dissatisfied as when they arrived, but they brought all the news I had for three long months.

At home the atmosphere was very bright and cheery, for Vere improved so quickly that she and Jim actually began to talk of marriage in the summer. The old doctor came up and croaked warnings when he heard of it. He said that Vere would need care for a long time to come, and that in his opinion it would be wiser to wait until she was perfectly strong—say a matter of two or three years longer; but Jim just laughed in his face, and said he flattered himself that he could take better care of his wife than anyone else could possibly do. So it was settled, and the astounding marvel has come to pass that Vere is so engrossed in thinking about Jim and their future life together, that she is comparatively indifferent to clothes. When I sounded her as to bridesmaids' costume, she said: "Oh, settle it yourself, dear. I don't mind, so long as you are pleased!" Two years ago she would have insisted on my wearing saffron, if it had been the fashionable colour, and have worried the whole household into fits about the shape of the sleeves! She is so loving and sweet to mother, too, not only in words, but in a hundred taking-pains kind of ways, and she never jeers or hurts my feelings as she used to do. Jim is going to have a very nice wife, and he deserves it, dear old patient thing!

In November, just as it was all settled about the wedding, Spencer came home from Malta, and stayed for a month. We were all simply bursting with pride over him, and the whole neighbourhood came up in batches to do obeisance. Why one should be prouder of a soldier who has never even seen a fight than of a nice, hard-working clerk, I can't think, but the fact remains that you *are*, and I did wish it were the fashion for Spencer to wear his lovely uniform, instead of a dull grey tweed suit like anybody else! The whole family was busy and happy and engrossed in the present. Nobody guessed what years those weeks seemed to me. I was quite bright all day long, but when I got to bed...

So the time went on, one day after another. Spencer went back to Malta, and Jim came down to stay for Christmas, also Lady Mary and her husband, and I sat up in my room making presents, and trying to live in the present and not look ahead. Then Christmas morning came, and among a stack of cards was a letter from Rachel—an extraordinary letter!

"I am quite well again," she wrote, "but mother is very frail, and takes cold at every change in the weather. Even this sheltered place seems too bleak for her, and we are seriously contemplating going abroad—not to the Continent, but a much longer journey—to South Africa itself! You may have heard that mother spent her early life at the Cape, and now that father has gone it is only natural that she should wish to spend her last years near her brothers and sisters. It will be a wrench for me to leave England, and all the dear friends who have been so kind to me, but I feel more and more strongly that it is the right thing to do. We shall try to sell the Grange, but shall, of course, come back for a few weeks after the New Year to pack up and make final arrangements, if, as I think probable, our plans are settled by that time."

The letter went on to discuss other subjects, but I could not bring my mind to attend to them. I just sat staring at that one paragraph, and reading it over again and again and again.

Going to the Cape! To spend her mother's last days! Mrs Greaves was not an old woman. She might easily live for another ten or fifteen years. Did Rachel seriously mean to imply that she herself was going to remain in South Africa all that time? And what about Will? Was he supposed to wait patiently until she returned, or to expatriate himself in order to join her? I felt utterly bewildered, and the worst of it was that there was no one near who could throw any light on the subject, or answer one of my questions. At one moment I felt indignant with Rachel for making no mention of Will's interest; at the next I marvelled how a mother, so kind and devoted as Mrs

Greaves, could possibly demand such a sacrifice of her daughter. What would Will say when the project was unfolded to him? After his long waiting he would be quite justified in taking a strong position and refusing to be put aside any longer. From what I knew of him, I fancied that he would do so—I hoped he would. Nothing could be more trying and dangerous for him or for me than a long, dragging engagement, with Rachel at the other side of the world—an engagement which held him bound, yet left him practically free.

I knew that Will was to spend Christmas at Bournemouth, and wondered if he would call on us on his return to discuss the astonishing news, but though father met him once or twice, he never came near the house until this morning, this wonderful never-to-be-forgotten morning when Bennett came to me as I was writing in the library and said that Mr Dudley had called to see me, and was waiting in the drawing-room.

To see me! Not mother, nor father, nor Vere, but me! My heart gave a great leap of excitement, and I trembled so violently that I could hardly walk across the floor. It must be something extraordinary indeed which brought Will on a special mission to me!

He was standing by the fireplace as I entered the room, and the moment he saw me he darted forward and seized my hands in both his. The last time we had met he would not even shake hands at parting. I remembered that with another thrill of excitement; then he drew me towards the fireplace and began speaking in quick, excited tones—

"Una, it is all over! Rachel has set me free! It is her own doing, entirely her own wish. I had no idea of it until Christmas Eve, when she sent me a letter telling me that she was going to South Africa with her mother, and could not continue our engagement. She asked me not to come to Bournemouth as arranged, but I went all the same. I could not accept a written word after all these years. I wanted to satisfy myself that she was in earnest."

"And was she?"

"Absolutely! I could not touch her decision—sweet and gentle and kindly as ever, but perfectly determined to end it once for all."

"Do you think that Mrs Greaves—"

"No, she has had nothing to do with it. The decision was as great a surprise to her as to me. She told me that she would never have consented to the South African scheme if Rachel had not first confided in her that she wished to break her engagement, and would be glad to be out of England. I think she is genuinely sorry. She and I were always good friends."

"Then why—why—why—"

"A matter of feeling entirely. Stay, I will give you her letter to read. It will explain better than I can, and there is nothing that she could mind your seeing."

He took an envelope from his coat pocket, unfolded the sheet of paper which it contained, and held it before me. I was so shaky and trembling that I don't think I could have held it myself. It was dated December 23rd, and on the first page Rachel spoke of the proposed journey in almost the same words which she had used in her letter to me, written on the same date. Then came the surprise.

"You will wonder, dear Will, if I am altogether forgetting you and your claims in the making of these plans; indeed, I never can be indifferent to anything which concerns your happiness, but I have something to say to you to-night which cannot longer be delayed. I am going to ask you to set me free from our engagement. I have come to the conclusion that I have been mistaken in many things, and that it would not be a right thing for me to become your wife. Please don't imagine that I am disappointed in you, or have any sins to lay to your charge. I am thankful to say that my affection and esteem are greater now than on the day when we were engaged, and I should be deeply grieved if I thought there could ever be anything approaching a quarrel between us. I want to be good, true friends, dear Will, but only friends—not lovers. I see now that I should never have allowed anything else, but you must be generous, dear, and forgive me, as you have already forgiven so many failings.

"Don't try to dissuade me. You know I am not given to rash decisions, and I have thought over nothing else than this step for some weeks past. I know I am right, and in the future you will see it too, however strangely it strikes you now. It would perhaps be better if you did not come here to-morrow as arranged—"

The rest of the letter I knew already, so I did not trouble to look at it, but turned back and read the last paragraphs for the second time, "I have been mistaken in many things!" "My affection is greater than on the day when we were engaged." "I have thought over nothing else for some weeks past." Those three sentences seemed to stand out from the rest, and to print themselves on my brain. I looked anxiously in Will's face, and saw in it joy, agitation, a wonderful tenderness, but no shadow of the suspicion which was tearing at my own heart. How blind men are sometimes, especially when they don't care to see!

"She has never loved me!" he declared. "She had, as she says, an affection for me as she might have had for a friend, a brother—an affection such as I had for her, but she does not know—we neither of us knew the meaning of—love!"

I looked at the carpet, and there rose before me a vision of Rachel's face when Will appeared unexpectedly on the scene; when she heard the tones of his voice in the distance; when she watched him out of sight after he had said "Good-bye." In his actual presence she was quiet and precise, but at these moments her eyes would shine with a deep glow of happiness, her lips would tremble, and her cheeks turn suddenly from white to pink. Not love him—Rachel not love Will! Why, she adored him! He was more to her than anything and everybody in the world put together. She might be able to deceive him, but nothing could make me believe that she had broken off the engagement for her own happiness. She was thinking of someone else, not herself. Who was it? Ah, that was the question. Her mother, or Will, Will and perhaps—me! Was it possible that she had been conscious of what had happened on the afternoon of the motor accident, and that, in consideration of our feelings, she had kept her own counsel until a sufficient time had elapsed to enable her to end her engagement in a natural manner? Anyone who knew Rachel as I do would realise in a flash that it was just exactly what she would do in the circumstances. Then, if this were indeed the case, the nervous shock which prostrated her for so long was not physical, but mental. Oh, poor Rachel! Yet you could smile at me, and be sweet and gentle in the first moments of your agony! It was all I could do to keep back the tears as I thought of what she must have endured during these last three months; but through all my agitation one determination remained unshaken: I must not let Will see my suspicions; Rachel's secret must be loyally guarded. He was talking incessantly—a quick, excited stream of words. I came back from my dreams to pick up a half-finished sentence—

"Too good to be true. She has filled so large a place in my life. I have such a strong admiration for her that it would have been a real pain to have parted coldly. But to keep her as my friend, to know that her affection is unchanged, and yet to be free to seek my own happiness is such a marvellous unravelling of the skein that I can hardly realise my good fortune. I came back last night, and could hardly wait until this morning to tell you my news. Una, you understand! I ask nothing of you to-day, it is not the time to speak of ourselves. I shall go back to my uncle, and stay with him for the next few months. He is very frail, and my place seems to be with him at present, but in the spring, if I come back in the spring, will you see me then? Will you let me tell you—"

I moved away from him hurriedly.

"No, no—don't say it! Say nothing to-day, but just 'Good-bye.' I don't want to think of the future—it's too soon. You said we must not think of ourselves."

"I did. You are quite right, but sometimes it is difficult to be consistent. You are not angry with me for coming to-day?"

He held out his hand as he spoke, and—I was inconsistent, too! I laid mine in it, and we stood with clasped fingers, quite still and silent for a long, long time, but I think we said many things to each other, all the same.

Then Will went away—my Will!—and I came upstairs to my room, and sat down all alone. No, that is not true—I can never fed alone now as long as I live!

Chapter Twenty Six.

January 20th.

Mrs Greaves and Rachel came home after the New Year and set to work at once to break up the old home. All the furniture is to be sold by auction, and the house is to be sold too, or let upon a very long lease. I wanted to see Rachel, but dreaded seeing her, at the same time, so at last I sent a letter asking when I might come, and she wrote back a dear little affectionate note fixing the very next afternoon. When I arrived she took me upstairs to the sitting-room where I used to spend my days when my ankle was bad, and fussed over me in just the same old way. She looked—different! Just as sweet, just as calm, but—oh, I can't describe it, as if something had gone which had been the mainspring of it all.

I should never have dared to mention Will, but she began almost at once to speak of the broken engagement, quite calmly and quietly, repeating that it was the best thing for both, and that she should be perfectly content if she were satisfied about Will's future.

"Nothing will give me greater pleasure than to hear that Will is happily married and settled down. He has been too long alone, and would so thoroughly appreciate a home of his own. I have done him a great injustice by condemning him to so many lonely years, but our engagement need be no hindrance now. It was known to very few people, and,"—she smiled a little sadly—"even those who did know refused to take it seriously. They saw at once what I was so slow in discovering—that we were unsuited to each other. We were thrown together at a time when he was depressed and lonely, otherwise the engagement could never have happened. It was a great mistake, but it is over now, and he must not suffer from its consequences. I am going away, but I shall wait to hear of his happiness, and I hope it may come soon."

Our eyes met. I looked at her steadily, and the colour rose in her cheeks and spread up to the roots of her hair. She shrank back in her chair and put up her hands as if to ward me off, but I just sank on my knees before them and held them tightly in mine.

"Oh, Rachel!" I cried. "I know, I know! You can't deceive me, dear. You have done this for our sakes, not your own. Oh, I hoped you had been too much engrossed to notice what happened that day. When you said nothing about it, I was so relieved and thankful, for truly, Rachel, it was only an impulse. Nothing of the sort had ever happened before—not a word or a look to which you could have objected. You believe that, don't you, dear? Say you believe it."

Her fingers tightened round mine.

"Indeed, indeed, I do! You have been all that is true and loyal, and so has Will. There is no one to blame but myself. I knew from the first that he was attracted to you, and that you suited him better than I could ever do; but I shut my eyes—I did not want to see. Don't be sorry for what happened; it is a great blessing for us all that I was not allowed to deceive myself any longer. You say it was only an impulse. Ah, Una, but the impulse which made him turn to you and forget me is too clear a warning to be neglected. It showed how his heart lay better than any deliberate action."

I could not deny it. I did not want to deny it, deeply as I felt for her suffering. I laid my head in her lap, so that she should not see my face, and begged her to forgive me.

"I feel such a wretch to take my happiness at the expense of yours. You are an angel, Rachel, to be so sweet and forgiving. I should be a fury of rage and jealousy if I were in your place, but you give it all up without a murmur."

She smiled at that—such a sad little smile.

"I have nothing to give. It was yours all the time. When I found that out, I could not be mean enough to hold an empty claim. I never meant you to know my real reason, but since you have found it out for yourself, you must promise me not to let it interfere with Will's happiness. Don't let me feel that he has to suffer any more because of me. Never let him suspect the truth. He has such a tender heart that it would trouble him sorely if he knew that I had discovered his secret, and I don't want any shadow on our friendship. Promise me, Una, that you will never let him know."

"I promise, Rachel. I had made up my mind about that long ago."

I did not tell her that in making my decision I had considered her feelings, not his. I had imagined that for her pride's sake she would not wish him to know her real reasons for breaking off the engagement. But Rachel herself had no thought of her pride; her anxiety was simply and wholly for Will's comfort.

I looked up at her in a passion of admiration, and in that moment a question which had tormented me for weeks past seemed to find its solution.

"Rachel," I cried, "I know now why this has happened! I have been wondering how anyone so good and unselfish as you could be allowed to have such a trouble as this, and how it could be for the best that you are passed over for a creature like me, but I can understand now. You are too valuable to be shut up in just one home; so many people need you—you can help so wonderfully all round that you are kept free for the general good. The world needs you. You belong to the world."

Her face lit up with happiness.

"Oh, Una, what a lovely thought! I shall remember that, and it will be such a comfort. Kiss me, dear. I am so glad that it is you. I am so thankful that Will has chosen someone whom I can love."

We talked a good deal more, and she said a lot of lovely things that I shall remember all my life. It was as though she were giving over the charge of Will into my hands, and they are such hasty incapable hands that they need all the guiding they can get. She told, me all about him as she had known him all these years—his good qualities, which I was to encourage; his weaknesses, which I was to discourage; his faults, (ah! Will dear, they were nothing compared to mine), which I was to help him to fight. She looked upon it all so seriously, that marriage seemed to become a terrible as well as a beautiful thing. Can it really be true that I have such wonderful power to influence Will for good or evil? Oh, I must be good, I must, I must, for his welfare is fifty thousand times dearer to me than my own!

After this I was constantly at the Grange, and worked like a charwoman helping to pack, and getting ready for the sale. I think I was really of use, for Rachel has not much taste, and I re-arranged things so that they looked ever so much more attractive, and so brought bigger prices. We had very happy times together, and were quite merry, sometimes sitting down to tea on the top of boxes, with our dresses pinned up and covered with aprons, but we never spoke of Will again. That was finished. The last two nights they were in England Mrs Greaves and Rachel spent in our home, and I drove down and saw them off at the station. I knew who was going to meet them at the other end, but even then we did not mention him. Rachel just clung tightly to me, and whispered "*Remember!*" and that said everything. Then the train puffed slowly out of the station, and I caught one glimpse of her white, white face through the window. Oh! if I live to be a hundred I shall never, never forget her, and I shall love her more than anyone else except my very own people, but I don't think I shall ever see Rachel again in this world!

June 25th.

Vere's wedding eve. My poor neglected diary must come out of hiding to hear the record of a time so wonderful to her and to me. I have had very little leisure for thinking of my own affairs since Rachel left, for a wedding means a tremendous amount of work and management, when it involves inviting relations from all parts of the world, buying as many clothes as if you were never expected to see a shop again, and choosing and furnishing a brand-new house. Neither mother nor Vere are strong enough to do much running about, so all the active preparations fell to me, and I had to go up to town to scold dressmakers and hurry up decorators, and threaten cabinet makers, and tell plumbers and ironmongers that they ought to be ashamed of themselves, and match patterns, and choose trimmings, and change things that wouldn't do, until Vere said, laughingly, that the wedding seemed far more mine than hers. It kept me so busy that I had no time to dream until I went to bed at nights and then I used to be awake for hours, thinking of Rachel away at the other side of the world, happy in her mother's restored health, and, to judge from the tone of her letters, thoroughly enjoying the complete change of scene after the very quiet life she had led these last years; thinking of Lorna, my dear old faithful Lorna, as good a friend to me as ever, in spite of all the trouble I caused her. It is a year ago now since that wretched affair, and Wallace seems almost his old self again, she says, so I hope he will soon have forgotten all about me. I feel hot and cold whenever I think about it. It is *wicked* to play at being in love! Suppose I had accepted Wallace out of pique, as I thought of doing for a few mad moments; suppose I had been going to marry him to-morrow—how awful, how perfectly awful I should feel now! How different from Vere, whose face looks so sweet and satisfied that it does one good to look at her.

I have been slaving all day long arranging flowers and presents, and after tea mother just insisted that I should come up to my room to rest for an hour, so here I am, sitting on the very same chair on which I sat in those far-away pre-historic ages when I began this diary, a silly bit of a girl just home from school. I am not so very ancient now as years go, but I have come through some big experiences, and to-day especially I feel full of all sorts of wonderful thoughts and resolutions, because to-morrow—to-morrow, Will is coming, and we shall meet again!

I think Vere guesses, I am almost sure that she does, for she and Jim made such a point of his coming to the wedding, and she gave me his note of acceptance with such a sympathetic little smile. Oh, how anxious I had been until that letter arrived, and now that it is all settled I can hardly rest until to-morrow. Rest! How can I rest? He arrives late to-night, so we shall meet first of all in church. I shall feel as if, like Vere, I am going to meet my bridegroom. It will seem like a double wedding—hers and mine.

The Wedding Day.

It has all passed off perfectly, without a single hitch or drawback. To begin with, the weather was ideal, just a typical warm June day, with the sky one deep, unclouded blue. As I looked out of my window this morning the lawns looked like stretches of green velvet, bordered with pink and cream, for it is to be a rose wedding, and the date was fixed to have them at their best. The house is full of visitors, and everybody seemed overflowing with sympathy and kindness.

It must be horrid to be married in a place where you are not known, or in a big town where a lot of strangers collect to stare at you, as if you were part of a show. This dear little place is, to a man, almost as much interested and excited as we are ourselves; the villagers are all friends, for either we have known them since they were babies, or they have known us since we were babies, which comes to the same thing. The old almshouse women had a tea yesterday, and sat in the gallery in church, and the Sunday-school children had a tea to-day, and lined the church path and scattered roses. The Mother's Meeting was in the gallery, too, and the Band of Hope somewhere else, and the Girls' Friendly by the door. The whole place was *en fête*, with penny flags hanging out of the cottage windows, and streamers tied across the High Street. It all felt so nice, and kind, and homey.

There were eight bridesmaids, and we really *did* look nice, in white chiffon dresses, shepherdess hats wreathed with roses, and long white staves wreathed with the same.

As for Vere, she was a vision of loveliness, all pink and white and gold. We walked together downstairs into the hall, where father was waiting to receive us. Poor father! the tears came into his eyes as he took her hand, and looked down at her. It must be hard to bring up a child, and go through all the anxiety and care and worry, and then, just when she is old enough to be a real companion, to have to give her up, and see her go away with a "perfect stranger," as Spencer says.

Last night, when I was going to bed, father held me in his arms, and said:

"Thank heaven, I shall have you left, Babs! It will be a long time before I can spare you to another man."

And I hugged him, and said nothing, for I knew... Ah! well, they did it themselves once on a time, so they can't be surprised!

The church was crowded with people, and everybody turned to stare at us as we came in, but I saw only one face—Will's face—with the light I most loved shining in his eyes. I stood at Vere's side, and heard her repeat her vows in sweet, firm tones, which never faltered, but Jim's voice trembled as he made that touching promise of faithfulness "in sickness and in health," and I saw his hand tighten over hers.

It was like a dream—the swelling bursts of music, the faces of the clergy; behind all, the great stained window, with the Christ looking down... Then the wedding march pealed out, we took our places in the carriages, and drove home once more.

Vere and her husband stood beneath one of the arches of the pergola, to receive the congratulations of their friends, a picture couple, as happy as they were handsome. The sky was like a dome of blue, the scent of roses was in the air, and Will came to meet me across the green, green grass.

"Una!" he cried. "*At last!*" and clasped my hand in his.

Oh, I am terribly happy! I should like everyone in the world to be as happy as I am to-day!

The End.

Printed in the United Kingdom by
Lightning Source UK Ltd., Milton Keynes
136965UK00001B/236/A